BGB

BLACK GRIFFIN BOOKS

Science Fiction and Fantasy

DOCTOR RAMANI'S CHILDREN

And Other Stories

G. S. Hargrave

Black Griffin Books

First Edition

Copyright © 2012 by G. S. Hargrave
Cover and interior design by author.

ISBN-10: 0615589960
ISBN-13: 978-0615589961

CONTENTS

Science fiction deals with improbable possibilities, fantasy with plausible impossibilities.

Miriam Allen de Ford, 1888-1975

When magic really works—and it sometimes does— it's probably just science not yet figured out.

Rachel, formerly known as TGF-48

Deep in the sun-searched growths the dragon-fly
Hangs like a blue thread loosened from the sky:
So this wing'd hour is dropt to us from above.
Oh! Clasp we to our hearts, for deathless dower,
This close-companioned inarticulate hour
When twofold silence was the song of love.

Dante Gabriel Rossetti, 1828-1882

DOCTOR RAMANI'S CHILDREN

O*donata-Anisoptera*," Dr. Ramani said, taking down a cage from the shelf. "That would be your common, garden-variety dragonfly." He put the cage on the lab table and switched on an inspection lamp. "This one is *anything but* common."

I bent over the fluorescent ring and peered down through the glowing lens. The greatly magnified insect rotated its head—most likely only reacting to the light, but giving me the odd impression that it was peering back up.

"I don't see anything unusual about it," I said.

"Nor would I expect you to, Captain Nakamura. But there have been changes—*modifications*—that only ten years ago I would have thought impossible." He gave me the sidelong glance of a sly old fox, dropping his voice to a conspiratorial whisper. "Of course, I said nothing of the sort. You don't talk about doubts when your research funding depends on optimism."

I kept a poker face. "So what does the Department of Defense actually get for its money?"

The old man smiled. "That, I imagine, is what *you're* here to find out."

He clicked off the lamp and returned the cage to its shelf. On other fluorescent-lit shelves below it were trays containing an assortment of terrestrial and aquatic plant specimens. As with the dragonfly, nothing seemed unusual about any of them.

"It's a fine afternoon," Dr. Ramani said. "Why don't we continue this outside?"

We took an elevator to the ground floor of the Center for Advanced Supercomputing and went out into the sunlight. Dr. Ramani led the way as we struck out across campus.

Central Illinois was a pleasant change from the heat and dust of Fort Hood, Texas. Overhead, white clouds were scattered across a blue summer sky like wandering sheep. Memories surfaced as we walked along—memories of how it had once been to be up among such clouds, and of how right it had once felt to have my hand on the control stick of the complex flying machine that is an Apache helicopter.

I caught myself and pushed the thoughts away. Only a year before, an exploding RPG and a splinter of Plexiglas had put a permanent end to all of that. An Army eye surgeon had told me later that I'd actually been quite lucky; from what I'd seen at the hospital in Germany, I knew that to be true. It was just that there had been a lot of days since when I'd had trouble looking at things that way.

Dodging oncoming students, we turned down a walk that led around an imposing botanical conservatory. Behind it was a water garden—a quiet little refuge centered on an ornamental lily pond. To the sides and back were scattered beds of purple irises. I caught their scent on the breeze. The far end of the garden was bounded by a line of willows, which seemed to follow the course of a hidden stream that led off campus. I could hear birds and the sound of running water from that direction.

Dr. Ramani nodded toward a bench that overlooked the pond. After a moment I realized why he'd chosen the spot: Dragonflies hovered and flashed in the sunlight.

"Beautiful, aren't they?" The old man smiled as he watched them. "I've always thought so. Even long ago, as a child in India." He turned on the bench to face me. "You were born here, Captain Nakamura?"

"San Francisco," I replied. "My parents came from Japan."

"Do you know the word *Akitsushima*?"

Shima signifies an island, of course, so the word was almost certainly a place name, but with *akitsu* I drew a blank. I said as much.

"*Akitsu* is an old Japanese word for *dragonfly*," Dr. Ramani said. "So, *Akitsushima*: Isle of Dragonflies. It's the name Japan was given in the time of your ancestors." He shrugged. "Such things often get lost with the passage of time. My own children know little of India. And my grandchildren?" He made an amused, dismissive gesture.

It was a complaint that I'd heard before.

"Do you speak Japanese, Doctor?"

Dr. Ramani shook his head. "A colleague does."

A swift, sunlit arc flashed through the air in front of us. Dr. Ramani's dark eyes followed. The dragonfly hovered just above the pond, its wings a silent blur against a water-mirrored image of sky and clouds. It delicately alighted on a

3

pink blossom.

Dr. Ramani watched the insect on its nodding stem. "Dragonflies were ideally suited to our purpose," he said. "They're quite large, as flying insects go. Their speed and agility on the wing are exceptional. And there's the compound eye: thirty-thousand facets, with an almost 360 degree field of vision. Wonderful little creatures, really."

The dragonfly took to the air again. Dr. Ramani's eyes shifted back to me. "Given the modifications that we intended, they were the perfect place to start."

"I'm not sure what you mean by *modifications*," I said. "Actually, I'm not even sure what I'm doing here. I'm a helicopter pilot."

He looked at me curiously. "What was it they told you?"

"That they needed someone with rotary wing experience for a project evaluation."

That was true enough, so far as it went, but there was a lot more I wasn't saying. Troubling questions had come up about Dr. Ramani's research project. Oversight under the previous administration, they told me, had been "shockingly lax," while progress reports over the past few years had become "increasingly vague." When money grows tight, the Department of Defense becomes a lot more particular about how it's spent. These days money was very tight indeed.

The bottom line was that I'd been given five days to figure out what Dr. Ramani was up to, and pointedly told to keep my eyes open.

Dr. Ramani was watching me closely. "There was something else?"

I shrugged. "They said I might find the assignment interesting."

He nodded, his silver hair shining in the sunlight. "Oh, I have very little doubt about *that*." He tipped his head toward the water lily, where another dragonfly had just come to rest. "How would you like to try flying one of those?"

* * *

What had Dr. Ramani meant by *modifications*?

In this case, he explained, it was what had happened when genetic engineering met nanotechnology. His dragonfly was the result.

The wings of Dr. Ramani's dragonfly were veined with conductive carbon filaments only a few atoms wide. These formed two invisible, virtually weightless antenna arrays, which were joined in the dragonfly's thorax to a radio transponder so tiny it could only be seen under the lens of a microscope.

The entire nervous system of the insect—from its three-lobed brain down to the cells of its ventral nerve cord—had been infiltrated by an intricate network of carbon nanowires. These joined into bundles of increasing size and complexity, to meet within the thorax at a nanobot-constructed microprocessor the size of a grain of rice. The microprocessor was linked to the transponder, and all was bio-electrically energized by way of a genetic redesign of the creature's nervous system.

I raised my eyebrows, genuinely impressed. "You're telling me that your dragonfly is some sort of remotely piloted aircraft? A *drone*?"

"I suppose that's how we've generally characterized it," Dr. Ramani replied.

"So they're thinking along the lines of a surveillance device. Maybe even a weapon . . ."

A look of annoyance crossed his face. "I'm afraid they do tend to view everything in terms of military applications."

"Does that surprise you? Dr. Ramani, we *are* talking about the Department of Defense."

"I have no interest in such things," he said. "Important research of the sort we've undertaken here costs a great deal of money, Captain Nakamura. I've looked on their funding as little more than a means to an end."

This certainly wasn't the sort of response that the people who had sent me would appreciate. What it sounded like to me was serious trouble.

Dr. Ramani was either oblivious or indifferent to that possibility. He obviously considered any discussion of practical military applications to be little more than a tedious digression, and quickly launched off again on the more esoteric aspects of his project. The wonders of his dragonfly didn't end with the fact that it was wired and flew wireless: Apparently it was also self-replicating.

"Your bug can make *another* bug?"

"Well, yes," Dr. Ramani said. "*Of course.* We designed it to be so from the start. That would be essential, wouldn't it? Owing to a dragonfly's brief life span."

"So how does *that* work?"

"All of the genetic modifications are passed on in the normal biological fashion," he said. "The nanobots that execute the non-organic elements of the design are themselves self-replicating, and are transmitted from organism to organism during the act of mating. All of the materials necessary to construct the microelectronic components are acquired from the dragonfly's local environment, by way of modifications made to the insect's normal feeding behavior."

It took me a moment to process all of that. My background in the biological sciences might not have gone beyond a handful of undergraduate courses before I'd entered the military and flight training, but an alarm bell sounded, nevertheless.

"Everything is self-propagating? Isn't that dangerous, Dr. Ramani? What would happen if your experiment got loose?"

"Very good!" he said, pleased. "That was one of the first concerns we had to deal with. Our solution was to build in a fail-safe mechanism: a transmissible code that throws a switch, so to speak. Mating behavior is turned off by default. It's only activated under carefully controlled conditions."

That sounded reasonable enough, I decided. After all, researchers routinely kept organisms that were far more dangerous than dragonflies in controlled environments.

"How many of your dragonflies are there?"

"At present, 124 adults," Dr. Ramani replied. He nodded toward the glass-and-steel structure at the front end of the water garden. "One hundred active breeders are isolated in a secure area of the botanical conservatory. Another 25 in non-breeding mode are generally at large in the local environment, where they're electronically tracked. Unfortunately, one of those was lost this morning. Terminal flight characteristics suggest that it was taken by a bird." He shrugged. "Not an uncommon event, I'm afraid, even for so alert and wary an insect."

I glanced around the garden, catching sight of dragonflies shining in the sunlight and resting quietly among the flowers. "Some of these are yours? Dr. Ramani's children?"

The phrase seemed to amuse him. "Almost certainly!" he said. "Although without the aid of a tracking device, even their own father will fail to recognize them."

That I'd been assigned to evaluate a questionable research and development program involving a miniature, remotely-piloted bionic aircraft wasn't exactly the sort of news that got my pilot's heart thumping. The fact that I'd most likely been sent to pull the plug on a kindly old man's pet project was altogether depressing. Still, I couldn't deny that my curiosity was up.

How, exactly, did one control the flight of an insect?

"What sort of operator interface have you got?" I asked.

"Something that's probably rather different from what you imagine," Dr. Ramani replied. "Tomorrow, if you like, we'll show you."

* * *

On the following morning I had my first sight of the project control room. There was a mechanical chair at the room's center. It looked like something you might expect to find in any dentist's office. The chair was surrounded by a U-shaped table, the top of which was cluttered with an assortment of flat-screen monitors and keyboards.

A tinted window filled the far wall, looking out across campus from the fifth floor of the Center for Advanced Supercomputing. I recognized the glass panes of the botanical conservatory roof shining in the distance. Beyond were the tops of the willows at the back of the water garden.

A fiber optic bundle as thick as my wrist snaked up from the floor behind the chair to the headrest.

"I don't see a display or controls," I said.

"The interface doesn't work that way." Dr. Ramani nodded toward a black plastic helmet resting on the table. "Have a look."

The helmet was surprisingly heavy. I turned it over, expecting an interior something like that of an AH-64D's integrated helmet system, complete with earphones, a microphone, and a heads-up display visor. What I expected wasn't even close. Inside was a padded, encircling headband, with a narrow midline support strap running front to back. What caught my attention, though, were the rounded golden contact pins. The interior of the hollow black hemisphere was a solid, gleaming mass of them.

"Neural sensors and stimulators," Dr. Ramani said.

Suddenly my pilot's heart *was* thumping. I had just sighted the leading edge of unexplored territory.

I turned at the sound of the control room door closing behind me. A striking young woman in a white lab coat was watching me over a stylish pair of glasses, which seemed to have a tendency to slip toward the end of her nose. Her dark hair was pulled back from her face and tied at the back. There seemed to be quite a lot of it.

"This is Captain Nakamura," Dr. Ramani said. "Joseph, Kohana Tanaka. Dr. Tanaka will be assisting us with a few initial adjustments this morning."

Apparently my status had changed at some point, from observer to participant. My interest level had changed, too.

"This could take a couple of hours," Dr. Tanaka was saying. Without missing a beat she shifted into Osaka-inflected Japanese. "Do you need to tend to anything before we begin?"

"There's no need," I replied, and threw in a polite bow for good measure. This, I realized, must be the colleague that Dr. Ramani had mentioned.

There was a hint of a smile as she gestured toward the chair. I sat. Curiosity satisfied, she switched back to English: "Please tilt your head forward, Captain Nakamura."

Dr. Ramani carefully positioned the helmet over my head. He steadied it with both hands as Dr. Tanaka did something at the back. There was a loud, hollow *click*. "Now," she said, "back."

I leaned my head against the rest. Motors hummed softly as the chair tilted into a partially reclined position.

Dr. Tanaka took a seat behind one of the terminals.

9

Dr. Ramani was already arranging himself at another. Both put on headsets as the overhead lights dimmed. A moment later I felt an almost imperceptible vibration of the helmet, followed by a slight metallic touch that spread out across the surface of my scalp in a wave.

"Please close your eyes," Dr. Tanaka said.

I watched the insides of my eyelids, clueless about what to expect. For a few minutes I listened to the sound of rapid keystrokes from Dr. Tanaka's direction.

"Have you noticed anything yet?" she asked.

At that precise moment a softly glowing spot of light appeared. When I tried to focus on the spot it skittered away, upward and to the right. "There's a white spot," I said. "Off-center. Right side, two o'clock."

"Good," Dr. Tanaka said. "I want you to follow it and tell me when it becomes stationary."

I played catch-the-spot for a while, until it finally became motionless at the center of my visual field. "Got it," I said.

We repeated the procedure with a second spot, superimposing it over the first.

There came more tapping at the keyboard. The spot stretched out upward and downward to become a softly glowing line. It was a bit odd, to be seeing something so clearly with both of my eyes closed.

"Now what?" Dr. Tanaka asked.

"A vertical line," I answered. "The top is tilted about 15 degrees left of center."

"Tell me when it's vertical."

The line slowly rotated clockwise. "Now," I said.

We repeated the steps with a horizontal line, and then superimposed the horizontal and vertical lines over the original center dot to form crosshairs. That was followed by softly glowing target rings centered on the dot, color balancing, and, finally, the resolution of a pair of outlined geometric figures into a simple stereoscopic image. An hour or so had passed by the time all at last vanished without a trace of afterimage.

"That went surprisingly well," Dr. Tanaka commented. "You just might be a natural." I heard keystrokes again. "OK, this next part is always fun. Hold onto your hat."

There were progressively subdividing squares, like a .gif image slowly appearing on the monitor of an old and dismally slow computer. Then the entire image suddenly brightened to full daylight intensity and snapped into sharp focus.

"What now, Captain Nakamura?"

For a moment I couldn't respond; the experience was too novel. My eyes were closed, but a mountain valley in winter spread out before me, filling my entire field of vision.

It was three-dimensional reality in freeze-frame—a life-size stereograph, capturing detail down to the smallest, motionless snowflake—except it wasn't *really* spread out before me; I was *inside of it.*

"You have *got* to be kidding," I said.

With another shock, I realized that the partial blindness in my left eye was gone.

"How is this possible?"

"A supercomputer has interfaced with your visual cortex," Dr. Ramani replied. "It's been busy from the moment you put on the helmet, mapping your neural pathways, analyzing their dynamics. It continues to do so even as we speak." I heard a few quick keystrokes from his direction. "It's presently becoming familiar with your auditory and speech centers."

I tapped the side of the helmet with a finger. "This thing

is safe?"

"You wouldn't be wearing it if it weren't." As Dr. Ramani spoke, I realized that another shift had just occurred: His voice now seemed to be coming both from his physical position across the room and from somewhere inside my head.

"The helmet involves a high-frequency, two-phase cycle," Dr. Ramani said. "During the stimulation phase, there are thousands of paired, low level electromagnetic impulses; targeted neurons fire at their focal points. During the reading phase, the helmet passively measures neural activity and feeds the data back to the computer. There's an enormously high rate of information exchange, but less radiation exposure than you'd receive from a cell phone."

The snow filled valley abruptly vanished. I opened my eyes, blinking, once again acutely aware of the lacuna marring my left-side peripheral vision.

"We've been concerned that some people might like it *too* much," Dr. Tanaka commented.

Evidently my enthusiasm was a little too obvious, although neither of them could have known the main reason for it. "This is how the dragonfly interface works?" I asked.

"You might find that experience somewhat more engaging," Dr. Ramani replied. "The operator interfaces with the computer, and the computer interfaces with the dragonfly—across the *entire* sensory spectrum." He turned the lights in the room up. "In effect, the operator *becomes* the dragonfly."

My head was teeming with questions, but one pushed to the fore: *"When can I try it?"*

The ghost of a smile flickered across Dr. Ramani's face. "We'll need to map your motor centers while you run through some computer generated flight simulations tomorrow," he said. "Assuming all of that goes well, perhaps the day after."

* * *

"I think Dr. Ramani might be having a go at matchmaking," Kohana Tanaka said, amused.

It was the evening of the third day. The two of us had apparently just been set up in a local Japanese restaurant.

I had met Dr. Ramani there for dinner. He'd said on the telephone that he wanted to go over the results of the day's flight simulations and to discuss what I might expect on the following morning. He and I had only been there for a few minutes when Dr. Tanaka had turned up—obviously much surprised to see me—and Dr. Ramani had left. He had received a suspiciously-timed cell call.

"I don't think I'd play poker with him," I said.

"Maybe you already are." Kohana smiled. "You do realize that your arrival here poses a problem for him. He's worried what sort of report you'll take back."

"I see." I casually picked up a shrimp with my standard-issue, Japanese restaurant *hashi*. "Are you part of his cunning strategy?"

She started to speak but suddenly stopped, looking down at her plate and—much to my surprise—blushing. "To tell you the truth," she said quietly, "that possibility hadn't even crossed my mind." She pursed her lips. "I'm afraid Dr. Ramani may be a devious old scoundrel."

"I already suspected as much," I said. "Although in this particular case, I probably won't hold it against him."

When she looked back up her expression had changed.

"The project has been very important to him, Joseph. I really do think he would have done almost anything to protect it. Now, though . . ." She looked at me uncertainly. "Well, I think he's worried that he may have done a deal

13

with the devil."

"The funding, you mean?"

She nodded. "When you take their money, you're supposed to give them what they want, aren't you?"

I thought back over the events of the day: The flight simulations had left me even more impressed than I'd been on the day before. I had quickly achieved control over a virtual dragonfly, navigating it at increasing speeds through geometric spaces of ever-increasing complexity. It was obviously the neural interface that the people at the Pentagon would see as important. It was easy to imagine the helmet's military applications: It could be adapted to control an aircraft or a missile; it could be central to an entirely new sort of deadly-accurate targeting system.

"But he *is* giving them what they want," I said. "Right?"

Kohana seemed about to speak—to say something she considered important, judging from her face—but she hesitated. She glanced away again. Then she casually pushed her hair back over her shoulders like a mass of black silk, and picked up her hashi.

I caught a hint of fragrance—something I should know—that touched lightly on a memory I couldn't quite pin down. The identity of the fragrance came to me after a moment: It was wisteria. The associated memory remained elusive.

It didn't occur to me until much later that she had never answered my question.

* * *

It was the fourth day. Dr. Ramani and I were alone in the control room.

"Won't Dr. Tanaka be here this morning?" I asked.

"She'll be joining us later," Dr. Ramani replied. He turned the second monitor so that he could see it from his place behind the first. "I'm sorry about last night, by the

14

way. The call was from the supercomputer lab. They ran across an anomalous transponder signal and thought I ought to have a look."

The lights dimmed. I could see reflections of the display screens glowing in Dr. Ramani's eyes.

"So what was it? Some sort of a problem?"

I wondered if he had heard me, but at last he shook his head. "Sorry. No, it was nothing that I hadn't anticipated."

The room became quiet. There was only the whisper of air from the vent overhead and the sound of Dr. Ramani quietly typing at the keyboard. I was comfortable in my semi-reclined position. My thoughts began to drift. I realized that I'd been thinking about Kohana Tanaka when the faint hum and vibration of the helmet snapped me back to the present. The contact pins were moving into position.

"Today will be rather different," Dr. Ramani was saying. "Initially the computer will simplify the sensory data, so your surroundings will seem much like yesterday's simulations. As we broaden the input spectrum, though, things will begin to change. We'll do that by degrees. There are transitional points that can be a little . . . unsettling. I want you to tell me if you begin to feel any disorientation. We'll leave it up to you to set the pace."

"Got it," I said.

"At the front of your right-side armrest, there's a lozenge-shape button on the underside."

I slid my hand forward and curled my fingers over the end of the armrest, finding the button.

"If you press it," Dr. Ramani said, "the interface will immediately shut down."

"Why would I want to do that?"

"No particular reason. It's just there if you want it." Dr. Ramani glanced at the monitor. "Your dragonfly is waiting

15

near the water garden, Captain. Are we ready?"

I closed my eyes.

The darkness shimmered and a glowing grid appeared. The grid pulled away and wrapped itself around me, defining the oddly extended visual field I'd first experienced during yesterday's flight simulations. It had been very peculiar, to find my peripheral vision not only restored, but extending well around toward the back of my head.

"You're in the sphere?"

"Yes," I replied.

"Very good. I'm initiating the dragonfly interface."

The grid vanished.

I was at the center of a world of simplified objects—all edges and outlines—moving slightly against a softly glowing background. There was a graceful, repetitive undulation all around me, synchronized with an odd physical sensation of gentle rising and falling.

"There's not enough detail," I said. "I can't make sense of any of this."

"I'm broadening the data spectrum now," Dr. Ramani said.

The glowing outlines faded; simultaneously the forms they had suggested took on increasing solidity. Colors began to emerge. Below me was a softly focused plane of yellow and green; high above, a blurry mass of pink, moving rhythmically against a field of luminous blue.

I became aware of a second sphere of sensations, separated from those external to myself by a bounding shape that felt utterly alien, yet strangely intimate and personal. With a shock I realized that I was experiencing the form of my host's body and the physical sensations of its bodily processes: a curious form of respiration; a twitch that was a wing movement; the slight flexing of a foreleg.

"OK," I said. "This is *definitely* getting weird."

"It's too much?" Dr. Ramani asked. "We could step it back down a little."

I couldn't decide if the sound of his voice was entirely inside my head now, or still outside in the control room. The very idea of a control room somehow seemed a bit strange and unreal.

"No, I'm fine," I said. "I'm having this odd sense of being in two places at once—like being between the waking world and a dream, and not being sure which is which. Just give me a minute to adjust."

I turned slightly, experimentally reorienting my dragonfly-self within its surroundings. It was only a matter of willing this to happen. Evidently the complex mechanics of movement were hardwired into the creature's nervous system.

"I think I'm ready for a little more," I said. "But *slowly*."

Soft focus gave way to gradually increasing clarity. The field of yellow and green below me became a floating lily pad of astonishing complexity, its surface a mosaic of living emerald cells; the moving pink blur above resolved into a blossom, nodding high against the sky at the end of a gracefully curving stem. The gentle undulations suffusing the environment were engendered by a procession of ripples rolling across the surface of the water, with each rise and fall echoed by a synchronized play of light, luminous shadow, and reflection. The air itself was a palpable medium, filled with myriad eddies and currents, alive with deeply meaningful vibrations, and awash with strange chemical messages.

My perception of time itself had changed. The speed of its passage seemed to ebb and flow, depending upon how I chose to direct my attention toward it. I felt as though I might descend endlessly into the depths of any passing moment if I wished to do so, and the wish to do so was very much present. It was an oddly seductive possibility.

"Are you still there, Joseph?"

"This . . . is a dragonfly's experience of the world?"

There was a pause before the answer came: "I would say both *yes* and *no*. It's *your* experience of a *dragonfly's* experience. Bearing in mind, of course, that this is no ordinary dragonfly. You're still receiving quite limited sensory inputs, by the way. I think the level you're at now should be quite enough."

"Somehow time seems different," I said.

"Time is as it has always been. You've just never experienced it this way before." A note of admonition came into Dr. Ramani's voice: *"Don't let yourself be drawn too deeply into the moment, Joseph.* Remember what Dr. Tanaka said about some people liking it too much? What you've just noticed is one of the things she was talking about."

An intriguing question popped into my head. "How does Dr. Tanaka know about that?"

"First-hand experience," Dr. Ramani replied. Before I could respond he spoke again: "We need to proceed to the next phase of our demonstration. Flight. Shall we attempt that now?"

"How do I . . . ?"

"You need only supply the intention," Dr. Ramani said. "Do you have to think about how to move your hand? Like your hand, the dragonfly will know what to do."

There was a vibration that I both heard and felt as the world suddenly dissolved into a blur of motion and color. When the petals of the pink blossom were again stationary, they were below me and to my left. I was hovering in the air.

"Very good!" Dr. Ramani said. "Now find out what you

can do. I'll tell you when it's time to return."

I rose toward the brilliance of the sun on humming wings, simultaneously watching the pink blossom as it rapidly fell away beneath me. In an instant I had taken up a position high over the water garden, even with the tops of the surrounding willows.

There was astonishing clarity in every direction. Depth perception was acute, except along an axis that ran directly from side to side, parallel with my vibrating wings. That, I realized, would be where the visual field of one eye didn't overlap that of the other. Peripheral vision was defined more by where on the visual sphere I chose to focus my attention than by bodily architecture or any optical limitations of the organs of sight.

Unexpectedly the sphere of the world tilted wildly and rolled around me, first one way and then the other. A dark shape flashed through the space I had occupied only a split second before. I saw it swiftly turning for another pass, but by then I'd already darted into the concealment of the nearest willow fronds and alighted upon a slender leaf.

The sudden gyrations had been reflexive evasions on the part of my dragonfly host. The wren, finding the air empty, flew off in another direction. I realized that the sensation of an accelerated heartbeat I was feeling belonged to my body back in the control room. The effects of the sudden expenditure of energy on my host had already subsided.

Dr. Ramani's startled voice entered my consciousness. *"What just happened?"*

"A wren," I said. "I think it's a dangerous world out here."

"It might be wise to stay out of the open for a while."

Good advice, I decided.

I dropped from my leaf, descended to the iris bed, dodged a surprised, pollen-covered bumble bee the size of a Volkswagen, and quickly abandoned the sunlight for the cooler spaces where willows followed along the hidden stream behind the conservatory. A short way in, the world was filled with the whispers and quiet gurgles of flowing water.

There was an approaching vibration on the air. My host responded instantly—as quickly as it had done with the wren—turning into the breeze to hover, while I frantically considered battle tactics with bumble bees.

No need. A second dragonfly hung in midair to my left.

"Good morning, Captain Nakamura." The voice in my head was that of Kohana Tanaka. Her dragonfly quickly dipped its wings left then right, bobbing once in the air—a signal any pilot would instantly recognize.

"There's another helmet!" I said.

"If you have some alternate explanation," she replied, "I would be very interested to hear about it."

"You might be a *kami*," I ventured.

The word—and the childhood memory that came with it—surprised me: I had spent a long-ago summer in rural Japan, visiting with my grandparents. One afternoon it had rained. As I had looked down from their mountain home onto a valley filled with swirling cloud, my grandmother had told me all about the kami spirits.

Another long-forgotten detail surfaced: There had been the scent of wisteria blossoms on the damp mountain air.

"Follow me," Kohana said.

Her dragonfly flew off down the stream, skimming close along the surface of the water, and launched upward through the green of overhanging willows toward a patch of blue. I followed close behind. We emerged from the treetops into the sunlight. I bounced on thermals as we crossed over the sun-warmed glass of the conservatory roof, and then dropped abruptly toward the cooler lawn far below.

"I keep hearing pinging tones," I said.

"External transponder signals," she replied. "Two pings tell you that you're leaving the range of one transponder and entering the range of another; a single ping tells you that you're about to lose your link."

"The transmission range is so limited?"

"Your onboard transponder is the size of a pinhead," she said. "It's powered by the bioelectric energy generated by an insect."

"So where are the external transponders?"

"Scattered all around us," she said.

It was a vague answer, but I was suddenly too involved with what was happening to think much about it. She banked hard to the right to follow along a sun-warmed sidewalk, taking advantage of the rising air to quickly gain altitude along the face of a building.

We were hovering in front of a tinted window, facing our own reflections. "Well?" she said.

It was the first time that I had considered my altered appearance. "Hey, I like the flashy racing stripes."

"That's not what I mean," she said. "Look *through* the reflection."

Interior details emerged. There was a man wearing a microphone headset. He was seated in front of a computer monitor with his back to the glass. Beyond was a second figure, reclining on a chair. He was wearing a black helmet.

Dr. Ramani turned toward the window. He seemed to be lip-synching along with the words that formed in my mind: "We should shut down the interface now, Captain Nakamura. It has already been nearly two hours. Your

21

dragonfly needs time to feed." He turned back to his keyboard and monitor. "When your vision goes dark, open your eyes and look outside."

I was suddenly in the chair. I opened my eyes and glanced toward the window, just in time to catch sight of a pair of dragonflies wheeling away into the sunlight.

The contact pins retracted as the lights came up. Dr. Ramani moved behind the chair to disconnect the cable. He seemed to be having a lot of trouble with the connector.

"Where's Kohana?" I asked.

"Down in the supercomputer lab," he said. There was a *click* as he finally got the cable free. As he took the helmet from me I noticed that his hands were shaking. His face had gone decidedly pale.

"Hey, are you alright, Doctor?"

"Not enough sleep, I think. I was in the supercomputer lab most of the night. If it's all the same to you, Joseph, I'll see you here in the morning. Dr. Tanaka should be along in a few minutes. Would you please tell her that I've gone home for the day?"

* * *

We were in the water garden. Kohana pocketed her cell phone and sat down beside me on the bench.

"He's at home," she said. "He promised me he'd get some rest. We're to start without him if he's late tomorrow."

"What happens tomorrow?"

"He wants you to learn to navigate the transponder net before you leave. It takes some practice to stay in range."

"I've been wondering about that," I said. "About the external transponders, I mean. I still haven't seen any."

"You won't. They're like the ones in the dragonflies, except they're photovoltaic. They're adapted to plants."

I remembered seeing the assorted plant specimens on

22

Dr. Ramani's shelves my first day in the lab—some aquatic, some terrestrial, and all likely part of a dragonfly's natural habitat. "They're also self-replicating?"

She nodded. "With transmission range so limited, we needed a way to establish an expanding transponder grid. We set out the first modified flora early on. Introduction had no apparent effect on the local ecology, so we decided to monitor the process and let it continue on its own."

Surprise and worry must have showed on my face.

"It's safe enough," she quickly added. "We could shut down replication across the entire grid at any time."

This was likely the same sort of fail-safe mechanism that Dr. Ramani had mentioned in connection with the dragonflies; a transmissible code, he had said.

She nodded in the direction of the stream. "By the end of last summer there was a continuous fifteen-mile transponder corridor. So far this summer, that's more than doubled. Surrounding woods and meadows are coming online; colonized areas are expanding and linking up."

Whatever the Department of Defense thought it was buying, I was fairly sure that it didn't include *this*. Truth be told, I wasn't even sure what the hell *this* was.

"Has Dr. Ramani told them about the limited transponder range?" I asked. "Or about the need for a pre-established grid?"

"All of the basic concepts were outlined in the original research proposal," she said. "There have been progress reports . . ."

I raised my eyebrows. "I suppose I should take that as a *no*."

She quickly looked away, but not before I caught the flash of anger that crossed her face.

"Listen, Kohana . . . I honestly don't see where he's got

23

a problem. I have no doubt that they'll see the neural interface as serious breakthrough technology. That *alone* should be enough to justify every Defense dollar he's taken— even if they think the dragonflies are totally useless."

"*Useless?*" She turned to face me. The anger was gone, but the disappointment that I saw in her eyes troubled me even more. "You really don't understand what *any* of this is about, do you?"

Obviously I didn't, but whatever I was missing seemed to be something that she wouldn't or couldn't explain.

Out across the water garden dragonflies flashed in the late afternoon sun. We had lapsed into silence, and the silence was growing long.

"What is it that you're afraid will happen?" I asked.

"I'm afraid that Dr. Ramani will lose control of the project," Kohana said. "I'm afraid that they'll take what he's accomplished, turn it into something destructive, and keep the rest locked away so it can't be used for anything else."

I had no answer to that. I had no clue what the *anything else* she was referring to might be, but the rest of what she said had sounded about right.

I would have felt better if she had simply gone with the anger. Apparently I was going to ruin something that I didn't even understand, and all I was getting from her because of it was resignation and sadness.

* * *

Dr. Ramani wasn't there when I arrived at the control room on the following morning. It was to be my final day with the project. My last day for a number of things.

Kohana looked tired. I commented on that, trying to find the easy familiarity of only a day before, but she responded only by saying that she hadn't slept well, and then fell silent. Eye contact was conspicuously absent.

I could read the signals well enough. They were telling me that any emotional connection between us was over. Most likely Kohana had concluded that this would be for the best. I was surprised by the sense of loss that came over me with the realization that she was probably right.

She waited for me to put on the helmet before coming around to attach the connector.

I was assigned a dragonfly, and quickly recognized my location on the stream just behind the water garden and conservatory.

"Where to?" I asked.

"South," Kohana's voice responded. "Just follow the stream. I'm going to let you go on your own for a while. Remember, two pings mean that you're moving from one transponder into the range of another; if you hear only one ping, you're moving completely out of range and are about to lose your interface."

I moved off downstream, skimming along the cool surface of the water, bouncing on the gentle updrafts that rose from sun-warmed rocks.

Barely audible double-pings—one low, one high—were frequent. After a while I began to get some sense of likely transponder locations: cattails, almost certainly; patches of algae and streaming water weed seemed likely, as did certain non-descript plants and weeds growing atop the banks. There was such profusion it was impossible to get an accurate idea of transponder range. To evaluate their usefulness, knowing the range was essential.

The obvious solution came to me. I turned into the breeze and rose against the wind into the air.

At treetop level nothing had changed. At around 150 feet I got a single low ping. That would be the internal transponder registering a weakening signal from the closest external source.

"What are you doing?" Kohana's voice asked. "Your signal strength is dropping."

"I know," I replied. I continued upward another 50 feet, and then another. Abruptly the world went dark. I opened my eyes on the dimly lit control room.

That would make the maximum range of the internal transponder only about 250 feet—roughly 100 feet beyond the single warning ping.

For almost any conceivable military application, that would represent a very serious limitation.

"Hold on," Kohana said. "I'll try to reacquire your dragonfly's signal." She studied the monitor for a moment. "Nope," she said. "His ID tag isn't lighting up. I'll have to find you a different ride." She looked up from the display. "Unless you want to try to flag one down yourself . . ."

"Say again?"

"You're wearing the helmet," she said. "It's linked to the computer, and the computer is linked to my microphone. You've got a similar connection with the transponder grid. How, exactly, are you hearing the sound of my voice?"

I thought about that for a moment. A memory suddenly came to me, of Dr. Ramani, seemingly lip synching with the sound of his voice in my head from the other side of a soundproof glass window.

What else might I hear by way of the helmet link, if I only listened?

Kohana saw it on my face when I got it. She smiled. I was surprised by how wonderful seeing her smile again felt to me. It was as if a weight had been lifted. For the moment, at least, we were back in the shared world of the project.

"It goes like this," she said. "Relax. Loosen your focus on the outside world and let your mind drift. Listen for the sound of a transponder tone. When you hear one, shift your total attention to that."

Eyes closed, I concentrated on my breathing, letting random thoughts pass by unattended. There came a moment when I realized that thought had stopped; it was an interval *between* thoughts. There were faint and distant tones in that moment, but the spell was broken by the very act of thinking about it.

I tried again. When the moment came—when the faint tones returned—I chose one and let go of everything else.

I was a dragonfly, hovering over an open meadow.

"Very good!" Kohana said. "Where are you?"

I wasn't sure, but something here seemed very different. There came a rush of exhilaration unlike anything I had ever felt. "I have no idea," I said, and the rush came again. I was suddenly struggling to keep up with a swelling flood of perceptions and sensations. "There's a meadow," I said. "Sunlight. Yellow flowers moving in the wind. There's a tree line along the edge. A river or stream over there, I think . . ."

"Hold on," Kohana said.

She was silent for the space of a few heartbeats, but it might have been for an hour. The glory of the world around me was rapidly escalating. Every flower, every stem, every blade of grass, and the very wind that moved them— *everything* was astonishingly alive. The *entire world* was alive, infused with consciousness, and drawing closer.

"You're about three miles south of campus," she said. "Just follow the stream north to get back."

"Kohana?" Suddenly I couldn't keep the panic out of my voice. *"Kohana? What's happening to me?"*

"Joseph?" There followed a pause that seemed to extend forever. It ended with the startled Japanese equivalent of *"Oh, shit!"*

27

A looming Presence had been about to speak to me. Now it was retreating, enfolding itself once again into the wind, the flowers and stems, the blades of grass.

"Is that better?" Kohana asked. "Joseph? *Are you OK?*"

I finally managed to frame a question with words: "What the hell just happened?"

"You interfaced at full sensory input level," she said. "For a moment I was reading some sort of anomalous transponder signal. I haven't got a clue where the breach in the buffer system might have come from." There was a pause. "Joseph? Do you want to terminate the interface?"

Did I want to terminate the interface?

I was aware that my body—the human body back in the laboratory—was still shaking. There was a button on the underside of the armrest, I remembered. But I needed time to process what I had just experienced. Time to work my way back to some semblance of normalcy.

"I'm OK," I said. "I need a while to think. I'll find my own way back to campus. Don't worry; I'm fine."

I crossed the meadow toward the trees and passed from sunlight into shade.

The stream was wider here, and running through a wilder place, but I instantly recognized it as the same stream that flowed behind the water garden and the botanical conservatory. It had the same . . . *presence*. For the space of half an hour I followed it northward.

I had much to reflect on, during that journey. On a meadow filled with yellow flowers a door had briefly opened, and I'd caught a fleeting glimpse of the unsuspected world that lay beyond it.

Perhaps the beliefs of Dr. Ramani's ancestors might provide some sort of frame of reference that would make sense of what I'd just experienced, I thought.

It hit me then that the beliefs of my own ancestors certainly did.

My grandmother had once told me about it.

* * *

As I came to the edge of the campus, Kohana spoke quietly inside my head. There was an odd tone to her voice. Something about it frightened me.

"Joseph? I . . . I just spoke with Dr. Ramani. He said you should come to the water garden. To the place where you were on the first day. OK?" There was a pause, then: "Joseph? I can't talk right now." There was a faint click.

"Kohana?"

Nothing. She had switched off her headset.

I followed the stream up to the edge of the water garden with an increasing feeling of foreboding, and came out into the full sunlight above the iris bed. Across the lawn, on the bench, I saw a slumped figure.

It was Dr. Ramani.

As I crossed the space between us my heart sank. Most likely the physical part of that feeling originated with my body back in the control room.

The old man was utterly still, his face expressionless, his lips slightly parted. His unfocused eyes were wide open, vacant, and fixed on nothing.

Perhaps, I thought, he had been watching his dragonflies when it had happened.

I alighted on his hand. And then I took to the air again, startled, when his finger twitched.

Dr. Ramani blinked. His eyes found and focused on me. He smiled.

"Ah . . . *Joseph.*"

Relief left me momentarily speechless. "You just scared the hell out of me, Doctor," I said at last.

Dr. Ramani's smile became uncertain. It vanished altogether as he figured out what my words had meant. "No, no, I'm quite well, as you can see! I was only away for a moment. I'm very sorry to have alarmed you!"

My mind was beginning to work again, and something else had just registered. "How did you recognize me?" I said. "*How can we even be talking?*"

"As a rule, scientists aren't supposed to become the subjects of their own experiments, Joseph. I'm afraid I've gone in for a lot of rule breaking lately." Dr. Ramani tapped the side of his head. "As you see, I have no further need for helmets or computers. I injected myself with nanobots the day after you arrived. They've been successfully adapted to the human genome." He smiled. "I've become part of the grid."

If I had known that he could, I probably would have guessed that he would. The man was undeniably brilliant—a genuine, once-in-a-millennium-level genius. What I hadn't decided was whether he was also a complete lunatic.

"Dr. Tanaka knew?" This seemed like a singularly important point, although I hadn't quite figured out why yet.

"Not until around ten minutes ago," Dr. Ramani replied. His face clouded. "I'm afraid dear Dr. Tanaka is very angry with me."

"She'll probably get over it," I offered weakly.

"Yes, she probably she will—since I don't seem to have killed myself." He paused, thoughtful. "I imagine she'll figure out the rest soon enough, if she hasn't already."

"The rest?"

"I released all of the dragonflies," he said. "I activated mating behavior and permanently deleted the code to stop it. Then I set the transponder flora to self-replicate and deleted their deactivation codes as well."

30

He smiled at me with the perfect innocence of a child.

"Do you understand, Joseph? *The door is wide open, and no one will ever be able to close it.*"

* * *

I was watching passing clouds through the window of a Boeing 737. For the past couple of days I had been in Washington, DC, presenting my report. Now I was an hour out from Dallas, en route back to Fort Hood. I wouldn't be staying there for long.

My term of enlistment was coming to an end. I'd had doubts about remaining in the service ever since I lost flight status, but I probably would have reenlisted. For some reason, I hadn't been able to imagine anything better waiting for a partially blind pilot out in the civilian world.

That inability, I suppose, had only been the result of a different sort of limited vision.

Nothing that I'd said in Washington had been untrue. No question they had asked me had gone unanswered. What I hadn't been asked about, though, I hadn't mentioned. It was a simple strategy, but one that had worked quite well.

They really liked what I had said about the helmet and the neural interface—so much so, in fact, that any questions about the disposition of research funds seemed to have been entirely forgotten. Kohana had been right about one thing: Someone else would be taking over Dr. Ramani's project. The part that the Department of Defense cared about, at least.

What little I had said about the dragonflies failed to generate much enthusiasm. I'd had a dull headache all of that day, so I suppose it's possible that my singularly lackluster account was partially to blame. In any case, once I had carefully detailed the extremely limited range of the

31

micro-transponders, they simply lost all interest.

Dr. Ramani couldn't have been happier with the outcome. He would likely be left alone now. The project funding would be gone, of course, but things were past the point where any additional funding would be needed.

Things, in fact, were well past the point of no return.

I asked Dr. Ramani about that, after I'd had time to sort out what he'd done and to think through all of the implications. He told me that important turning points in human history have always carried elements of risk, and that failure to take them can sometimes be the greatest risk of all. *Someone* had to decide, and that responsibility had fallen to him. He said that to decide had been his *duty*.

While Kohana had been shocked by her colleague's actions, she was also very much in awe of his vision and audacity. There had been no negative environmental consequences observed over several years, she reminded me. Profound changes *were* coming, but the dangers they held most likely wouldn't be on that level.

Every human being would soon be presented with an astonishing new potential. Their descendants would have that potential as a rightful inheritance. Each could choose whether to step through the doorway or not. It all came down to the dangers inherent in an individual's freedom to make choices.

I'd made my own decision before I left for Washington. The headaches had soon passed, just as Dr. Ramani said they would. While I haven't heard a ping yet, I've been a long way beyond the transponder grid's current range. That range is rapidly expanding. In the meantime, I'll soon be taking up residence near the university.

As Dr. Ramani has observed, universities have always been very good places to point toward newly opened doors.

BD-428

They were seven plus one—the seven being soldiers, and the one an ambulating, four-legged machine.

They were hurrying along a high mountain path, just coming to a place where it bent out of sight around a fold in the steep stony face, when there was a blinding flash and a simultaneous blast of heat and pressure.

Catastrophe had come in an instant. The sound of it carried for miles, rebounding off towering walls of rock and echoing through deep, desolate valleys.

* * *

Nelson opened his eyes and blinked up at the sun, uncertain where he was. The air was hot and full of acrid smoke. He rolled onto his side and coughed, and the pain that this caused astonished him. After a moment, he blindly groped in the dust for the strap of his pulse weapon. Then he managed to sit up and look around.

What he saw was appalling.

Everyone else was dead. There was simply no question of it. Those who hadn't been swept over the precipice by the blast were scattered along the path, their dull black armor broken. They had been reduced to heaps of tattered cloth and smoking plastic, and Nelson couldn't even tell for sure how many were there.

That he should still be alive himself seemed utterly impossible.

The man who had apparently done this came through the smoke just then. In one hand he held what looked like a garage door opener, though there were no such doors to be opened around here. An AK-47 hung by a strap from one shoulder.

The man was shouting excitedly into a small handheld device. He showed no caution whatsoever. He, too, must have thought it impossible that anyone could have lived.

There were shrieking flashes of light as the man and his weapon disintegrated. Any surprise he had felt when he had suddenly glimpsed something moving among the scattered debris had been entirely momentary.

Nelson flipped the pulse rifle butt-to-the-ground and clambered up by slow degrees, gripping the weapon with one hand for support and clutching his side with the other.

For a moment he just stood there, shaking and dizzy, ears ringing, trying to sort things out. He absently glanced down at his palm. There was no blood, but he guessed from the throbbing in his side that some ribs might be broken. The smooth hard shell of his form-fitting nanofiber carbon body armor was cracked. That certainly signified something.

He looked through the smoke toward the place where the man had appeared. Whoever the man had been talking to would have heard the howl of Nelson's pulse rifle, over the open com link at the very least.

Nelson wheeled and targeted an unexpected sound behind him, nearly cutting loose again before he identified its source: It was BD-428, awkwardly regaining its feet.

BD-428 was the squad's new *plus one*—their all terrain, cargo-carrying robotic quadruped. The machine looked like a cross between a headless mechanical mule and a flat-black, four-legged spider.

This had been its first time in the field. They had thought to use a routine patrol as an initial shake-down outing, but *routine* wasn't what had happened.

BD-428 was wobbling, trying to regain its balance. One side of its camo cargo tarp was scorched and smoking.

BD-428 had been walking between his own position and the IED at the moment it had detonated, Nelson realized. The robot's squat black shell had deflected the main force of the blast. That was how he had survived.

Nelson found his helmet. It had taken a serious hit, but it powered back up when he put it on. The com link and GPS were gone, but the optical system seemed to still be fully functional.

He lowered the visor, looked past the bend to the place where the trail reappeared, and followed it out along the side of the mountain into the distance.

Tiny figures were there, shimmering in the heat.

A couple of carefully timed blinks stabilized the image and increased the helmet's magnification.

The figures were insurgents. They were moving rapidly along the trail in Nelson's direction.

A totally unexpected, province-wide offensive had begun yesterday. All of that day Nelson's squad had been hotly pursued. This morning they thought that they had finally gained some breathing room, thanks to their night vision equipment. Now Nelson saw that their hope of escape had been an illusion. Unknowingly, they'd also been cut off to the front—trapped on the steeply rising trail between a sheer drop to the left, a vertical wall of stone on the right, and closing enemy forces.

Nelson looked up the rocky cliff face, his visor automatically darkening against the blinding intensity of the sun. Ascent looked perilous, but the decision couldn't have been simpler: If he stayed where he was, he was dead.

There was little time to think things through. One by one Nelson gathered up his squad mates' weapons and sent them spinning over the rim to clatter faintly against the rocks far below. The gathering up was grim business. He tried not to look too closely, but he couldn't help what he saw.

Salvaging a fully functional helmet was out of the question. Quick, disturbing glances showed there was simply nothing left to salvage.

He numbly wiped off his hands when he was done.

Experimentally he took a deep breath. Pain flashed around his side, but at least there was no sensation of anything moving that shouldn't be. He activated his combat rig's Emergency Medical Pack and hit a couple of buttons. The pain dulled with a transdermal jet of synthetic opiates, as his energy level surged with a double-dose of stimulants. The opposing mix of drugs felt dangerous as hell, given what he was about to attempt, but that seemed totally irrelevant at the moment.

Nelson slung the pulse rife diagonally across his back. He gritted his teeth and jerked the strap down tight. Face grim, he began to climb.

* * *

One-hundred meters up, drenched in sweat and close

to the point of collapse, Nelson was almost within reach of the narrow ledge that he had seen from the path far below. Through a swimming haze of approaching heatstroke he heard slipping rocks and the rattle of a malfunctioning servo valve below him.

BD-428 was trying to follow.

Nelson probably would have expected the robot to try, if he'd had a moment to think about it. Following was what BD did. But attempting to follow was one thing; actually scaling a near-vertical wall to do so was quite another.

Nelson had just gotten a hand over the rim when a bullet whined past his head like an ascending, hypersonic hornet. A split-second later came the *crack* of the shot from below. He desperately groped for purchase. Abruptly stone chips exploded into the air all around him, and something glanced hard off his body armor.

He heaved himself over the edge and frantically scooted backward until his pulse rifle slammed into solid rock. The resultant jolt of agony was outrageous, even through the cottony padding of EM pack pain-killers.

BD came into view, shuddering under a furious hail of automatic weapons fire. The locals hated the robots. They hated their weird semblance of life. They considered them unholy abominations.

BD's hydraulic legs were splayed wide, the dull black shell of its undercarriage scraping against stone. It awkwardly rocked itself over the rim and scrambled for cover.

"Hey, Big Dog," said Nelson.

Nelson's throat was so dry that the words nearly choked him. He found that he couldn't swallow. Suddenly bright spots were flashing before his eyes and his heart was racing like a trip-hammer, dangerously skipping beats.

He fumbled desperately at the EM pack with a badly shaking hand, cutting the flow of stimulants, and then sucked hot water through his hydration tube, letting it trickle down his throat until he could gulp down a few mouthfuls. He closed his eyes and dropped his head back against the vertical stone. He focused on taking slow, regular breaths.

It took long minutes for his vision to clear, for his heart to gradually slow, for its rhythm to steady to a point where he no longer thought it might burst or simply stop. As the sense of impending death subsided, clarity slowly returned.

He had evaded his pursuers. He had slipped from between the closing pincers and was still alive. If he made no mistakes, there was a slim possibility that this state of affairs might continue.

Nelson inched forward, pulling his weapon by the strap, and cautiously peeked over the rim.

Nothing down there was moving. He closed his eyes again, trying to gain calm and focus.

Suddenly he popped up into a low crouch and directed a howling stream of fire downward, sweeping back and forth across the entire exposed area. The squat black weapon launched a swift stream of accelerating, gyroscopically stabilized rockets, each gaining kinetic energy until the moment of incandescent impact. Stones whined off into space like shrapnel as an enormous cloud of dust gathered and rolled, illuminated by bright, pulsing flashes.

Nelson dropped back to the wall, trying not to think about the bodies he'd left behind, or of what else he had probably just done to them. It had been necessary. A pulse rifle running full-bore made for a terrifying display of force. No sane man would be thinking about scaling the cliff anytime soon. Time was what he needed.

He gulped down more water as he carefully examined his surroundings. Loss of his com link meant no topographic display, but the ledge he'd attained certainly looked like a path. It was most likely the *same* path. To the left it descended, quickly disappearing from view. That immediately worried him. To the right it climbed.

Up was good. Up and over, then down the opposite side of the mountain toward the safety of Firebase Tango. That was where the squad had been headed, before disaster had overtaken them. It was still a plan.

Nelson gave Big Dog a quick inspection. The left rear leg and the undercarriage of the machine were slick with oily red hydraulic fluid. A heavy drop fell to the ground as he watched.

BD, Nelson thought. *Bleeding Dog.*

"How are you doin' there, Big Dog?"

There was no response, of course. BD transports had come with Verbal Command and Response beginning with the 300 series, but it wasn't likely that the new 400's enhancements included improved conversational skills.

Nelson knew the magic words: "BD-428. Operational status. Report."

The response came in the unaffected voice of a no-nonsense military machine: "BD-428. Damage, upper left rear actuator cylinder; system compensating with diminished load capacity. Hydraulic pressure, 70 percent. Power remaining, 10 percent. Recharge system active. Estimated time for full recharge, 4 hours, 32 minutes."

Broken Dog, thought Nelson.

Yet it had made the impossible climb, carrying the squad's store of supplies and ammunition. For that small miracle, Nelson was enormously grateful. He would need some of the supplies. His survival would depend on them.

There was no waiting here while the Stirling Radioisotope Generator slowly recharged the transport's batteries. That was a given. Nelson had to move. The uphill climb would drain power far more quickly than the SRG charger module could replace it.

"Well BD, we sure as hell can't hang around here." Nelson glanced at the machine. "Logic tells me you're not going to make it. I don't suppose *you* have any bright ideas."

"BD-428," said the voice. "Enhanced logic capabilities available. Select Operational Intelligence Parameters for menu."

The response was entirely unexpected. The new 400 model was pretty much an unknown quantity. "Operational intelligence parameters?"

The machine seemed to take that as a command. "BD-428. Operational Intelligence Parameters. Current setting: Level One, Personnel-Following All Terrain Transport Unit. Available settings: Level Two, Autonomous GPS-guided Transport Unit; Level Three, Autonomous GPS-guided Transport Unit, with Tactics Logic. Please identify command authority and select a setting."

"I'll be damned," said Nelson.

"Please identify command authority and select a setting," the machine repeated.

Command authority? Nelson made a guess: "Nelson, Richard A." Nothing happened, so he added his rank and serial number.

"Nelson, Richard A. Command authority acknowledged. Please select a setting."

"Level Three," said Nelson. What the hell? Higher was generally better.

"Level Three," BD announced. "Autonomous GPS-guided Transport Unit with Tactics Logic. Selection

40

engaged."

And that seemed to be the end of that. Nelson wasn't sure what had just been accomplished, if anything.

Time was passing. Nelson glanced back down the falling path to his left, his uneasiness growing. Out here, finely-tuned paranoia tended to have definite survival value. He had to get moving.

The transport could still be useful, at least for a while. BD's remaining power would undoubtedly last longer if the cargo were reduced. Nelson turned back the dusty tarp.

Most of the rations could go. He simply dumped them over the rim. Anyone bothering to gather them up would be slowed down by doing so. Most of the water that hadn't been lost in the blast could go, too; the supply had been meant for seven, but now there was one. Nelson threw off all but two of the plastic bladders. He slashed those he discarded to spill out over the hot stones. He kept a good supply of ammunition, but heaped the bulk alongside the trail. He considered leaving a grenade, pin pulled, under the stack, but quickly thought better of it. His pursuers lacked pulse weapons, so the ammo would be useless to them; they would be wary of whatever he might abandon, but some other poor fool might not be.

Nelson slung the pulse rifle back onto his shoulder. "Time to go, BD."

"BD-428. Operational Intelligence Parameters, Level Three. Please state destination."

It took a moment but Nelson got it: *Personnel-Following* was now out of the mix. BD required an objective.

"Firebase Tango," Nelson said.

"Destination coordinates acquired. Recharge cycle incomplete. Power remaining, 10 percent. The destination is beyond current operational range. Shall I proceed?"

41

Nelson raised his eyebrows. To be questioned by a piece of talking equipment that was suddenly referring to itself with a first-person pronoun was definitely a little weird.

"*Yes*," Nelson said. "*Proceed*. People are coming to *kill* us."

"What is their estimated time of arrival?"

And getting weirder by the moment, Nelson thought. Of course, he'd recently dosed himself with a potent mix of psycho-active chemicals.

"I don't know," Nelson said. "*Soon*."

There was an unsettling pause—a little too much like a moment of thought, perhaps.

"BD-428," said the machine. "Operational Intelligence Parameters, Level Three. Mission objectives reprioritized."

The hum of the compressor motor rose. BD started up the trail, rocking from side to side like an injured mountain goat. Or maybe like an injured spider? The rattling wasn't so bad now, at least. Lightening the load had helped.

Nelson glanced nervously down the descending path again, and then turned to follow BD-428 upward.

* * *

The narrow and steeply ascending switchback trail made for a precarious climb, with frequent dizzying views down the rocky face of the mountain to the sun-blasted flats far below. By mid-afternoon, climbing was like walking through a furnace. The world seemed to ripple. There was no shade, and any slight stirring of the air was only from its rising with the increasing intensity of the heat.

Sweat stung Nelson's eyes fiercely—flash burns from the blast, he supposed. The water he sucked through his hydration tube to make up for his rapid losses might have been coming from a hot thermos, instead of the vest-like bag beneath his nanofiber carbon armor. It was beneath the

42

armor to keep it from freezing, he'd been told. Some great idea, in a furnace like this. The water tasted of hot plastic.

Nelson had been stopping periodically to look down over the edge, whenever they had come to good vantage points. Twice he'd seen pursuing figures on the trail far below. There were six that he'd counted, moving along quickly in good military order. He paused again now, looking back and down across a kilometer or so of empty space.

His pursuers were there, climbing the trail in the opposite direction, approaching the point where Nelson's ascent had reversed only an hour before. While out of his sight they had rapidly closed the distance. Nelson saw that one of the tiny figures had paused, dropping behind the others. He lowered his visor and zoomed in for a closer look.

The man who had stopped was looking back at him through powerful binoculars. He tapped the binoculars significantly with a long brown finger and then slowly lowered them, keeping his eyes fixed on Nelson's position.

The keen, unblinking stare and lean angular face reminded Nelson of a bird of prey. Of a falcon, Nelson thought, totally focused on the hunt, waiting for the moment when it could strike.

* * *

The final upward stretch was the worst. Afternoon had turned to evening; the intensity of the heat was beginning to lessen, but the last of Nelson's strength was nearly spent. The pitch of the transport's compressor motor was dropping, too. BD's power would soon be gone.

Nelson hadn't glimpsed the enemy for over an hour, but he knew they were close. That was all that kept him moving.

As he neared the end of the climb, he considered laying an ambush. The pulse rifle was his single advantage; with the right set-up, that could be more than enough.

43

He abandoned the hopeful notion the moment he topped the rim. Just beyond it, the terrain was flat and open. It fell away to the east, his intended direction of travel. There were no places of cover and concealment out there, while the rim would provide his pursuers with a convenient line of protected firing positions.

Waiting on the rim itself made no sense, either. He would be a clearly visible silhouette against the sky, with the late day sun in his own eyes.

Either position would essentially put him on the wrong end of a shooting gallery.

"BD-428," Nelson said. "Operational status. Report."

BD's response was altogether dismal: "BD-428. Current Operational Intelligence Parameter Setting, Level Three. Line-of-sight distance from objective, 20.25 kilometers. Damage, upper left rear actuator cylinder; system compensating with diminished load capacity. Hydraulic pressure, 60 percent. Power remaining, 3 percent. Estimated time to system shut-down, 30 minutes. Recharge system active. Estimated time for full recharge, 6 hours, 45 minutes."

The long climb had really knocked down BD's batteries; Broken Dog was definitely on borrowed time. Nelson knew that he was too, if he didn't start moving again.

"We can't stop," Nelson said. "The enemy is coming. They're very close now."

"BD-428. Optimal course to destination plotted." BD set out a few points off of due east, without hesitation or further comment.

BD has GPS, Nelson thought. *BD has a map in his head.* Although—strictly speaking—BD had nothing like a head at all.

Fatigue was taking its toll, Nelson realized. His brain

44

was rapidly running down, just like BD's batteries.

He wearily shouldered his weapon and began walking. He concentrated on the simple matter of putting one heavy, dusty boot in front of the other; on dragging along behind the leading transport unit and watching his own rapidly lengthening shadow

* * *

There was a winding gully that descended eastward, first cut through the ancient rock when the climate here had been very different, and then slowly deepened by untold thousands of years of infrequent rain. Nelson thought vaguely of that as the gully first came into view, but his thinking soon turned to the concealment it would provide on an otherwise featureless landscape.

BD had found it, and then BD had found the way in. Nelson wondered what machine logic might be at work. Most likely it was only a matter of topographic data and GPS navigation. Firebase Tango, still nearly 15 kilometers distant, was at the bottom of a broad, arid valley, situated on what in this godforsaken place passed for a river. Probably the gully would be making for there along the shortest and easiest path—the course that long-vanished water had once followed. That same shortest and easiest path was all that mattered to a robotic navigation system.

The shortest path was far from straight, and being strewn with rocks and boulders it was far from easy. The gully deepened as they progressed. Soon Nelson's shadow was lost in the gathering gloom. Only the rims on either side still caught the sun, remaining brightly lit against dark stone and a sky turning from a peacock blue to violet. Venus had just risen to the east. It hung low in the darkening sky, shining like a jewel.

It was beautiful beyond words, but the sight of it made

Nelson feel utterly alone.

A kilometer or so in, the inevitable moment came. The pitch of BD's compressor motor had already become a labored growl. Now it stopped altogether, and the world at the bottom of the gully was suddenly still. Nelson staggered up even with the transport unit.

"BD-428," the robotic voice said. "Power level critical. Estimated time to full recharge, 7 hours. System shutdown in 1 minute."

"OK, BD," said Nelson. "You've done well." He wasn't sure why he added that, but it somehow seemed right. "I think we're out of options."

"BD-428," said the voice, oddly hollow in the silence of the gully. "Operational Intelligence Parameters, Level Three. Unit auto-destruct sequence is available."

Nelson stood there, staring blankly at the dark outline of the machine, wondering for a moment what it was he'd said that had prompted the last comment. "What's the auto-destruct damage radius, BD?"

"Auto-destruct damage radius, zero meters," BD replied.

Nelson understood. No doubt it was part of the enhanced series 400 package. You could render disabled equipment totally useless before you abandoned it on the field. You could stand safely alongside as you did so.

For some unaccountable reason, Nelson was suddenly furious.

He glanced around their immediate surroundings. A few meters away, against the wall of the gully, was a large boulder that had collected a pile of tumbled rocks. To one side was a recessed area of deep shadow. He looked down. The gully floor was stone. Their movements left few traces.

"Forget the auto-destruct sequence," Nelson said. "Got

46

that? *Do not auto-destruct.*"

BD-428 had just enough remaining power to make it to the place of concealment and hunker down as commanded. Nelson hurriedly refilled his hydration bag and filled a couple of plastic canteens for good measure. He dumped the remaining water BD carried onto the ground. It spread over the dim, parched stone and vanished in a heartbeat.

"OK," Nelson said. "Stay here until you've got a charge up. Then continue to Firebase Tango. That's your mission, BD. That's my final order."

Nelson pulled the dusty tarp that had covered BD's load over the side of the machine. In the growing darkness, BD would soon be invisible.

Nelson turned and continued on down the gully, dismissing any thoughts about why he'd just wasted valuable minutes.

* * *

An hour later, as the interior of the gully was becoming too dark to navigate, Nelson discovered that his damaged helmet's night vision was gone. There would be the light of a first-quarter moon, but that wouldn't be for a couple of hours.

Nelson tried to collect his thoughts. He could get badly needed rest, knowing that his pursuers also lacked night vision equipment. Somewhere back along the gully they would be equally blind. Of course, they might be following above, along the flat gully rim. They might keep closing the distance in the better light up there while he rested. But only to a point.

The man with the binoculars had looked intelligent and experienced, Nelson remembered. That one would know the risk of walking into an ambush, or of passing their quarry in the dark to be cut down later from the behind.

47

G. S. HARGRAVE

They couldn't know for sure how far he had come since he'd started down the gully. For the past hour, they hadn't even had the rattle of BD's malfunctioning servo to listen for.

If *I* were the hunter, Nelson thought, I'd close the distance for a while, but stop well short of my quarry's estimated position. Then I'd begin moving again by moonlight. I'd have two men coming down the floor of the gully and two following along each rim above. That would cover all bases, and make best use of the high ground by providing for a deadly crossfire. I'd figure on interception and a kill sometime just after sunrise.

Nelson set his watch for 2 hours and closed his eyes.

No time at all seemed to pass before he felt the vibration of the watch on his wrist. He opened his eyes on a narrow, bolder-strewn world of moonlight and shadow.

His thinking was clearer now. Even a little sleep had helped. He got up and started walking.

* * *

Shortly after sunrise they caught him, at a place where the walls began to fall away as the gully broadened out from the foot of the mountain. A poorly aimed shot rang out, blasting up dust and stones just ahead of him. Nelson launched himself over a low-lying rock into cover. Firebase Tango had been only a couple more kilometers ahead, downhill and just over a ridge, almost in sight. Now that was two kilometers too far.

He was trapped.

As he had anticipated, there were two on the right and two on the left, glimpsed in their crouched runs along the opposing rims. The two he'd expected to come up the middle were so far missing, but those he'd already spotted would be more than enough. They would quickly improve their

48

positions. Behind him, the long slope down toward Firebase Tango provided them with an open field of fire. Any break in that direction would make him an immediate target.

One of his pursuers would soon try for a firing position between himself and the firebase, Nelson knew, moving in a wide, unseen loop from one side or the other. Once the maneuver had been accomplished, that would be that.

Nelson glanced down the long slope that led to safety. It was a suicidal move, but the only option remaining.

He punched a button on his EM pack and punched it again; the effect was a time-altering rush. He sprang up, raked both rims with his pulse rifle, turned downhill, and ran like hell.

One hundred meters on, something slammed his left shoulder like hard-swung bat, spinning him completely around. The pulse rifle flew away, striking the ground with a clatter, while Nelson hit flat on his back in a shallow depression.

He was looking up at the morning sky, impossibly clear and bright. He could feel the life pouring out of him, the warm flood of it pooling all around his back, rapidly flowing along the backs of his arms and legs. There was little pain to speak of, really; only numbness.

I'll bleed out before they get here, he thought.

It seemed like a very long wait, but Nelson didn't mind. He just watched the sky. Somewhere he could hear the faint hum of a distant motor: Firebase Tango, the place that had been too far . . .

At last he heard footsteps on gravel.

Four men were looking down at him. One was the man with the binoculars—the Falcon Man. His face was grim, but Nelson saw no hatred there. The man was readying his rifle. Then his head jerked up.

49

It was the motor again, but much closer now. Suddenly it pitched to a rising, rattling whine, accelerating down the final stretch of gully out onto the slope. The sun was blotted out for an instant. Bodies flew like bowling pins. There followed a brief confusion of shouts, wildly fired shots, spinning shapes and horribly cracking thumps, then the pitch of the motor dropped to a hum. It approached and stopped nearby.

Nelson smiled weakly up at the sky, blinking against the settling dust. "BD-428," he said. "Report."

"BD-428," said the robotic voice. "Level Three. Autonomous GPS-guided Transport Unit with Tactics Logic."

BD-428 had been repeating those seemingly innocuous words since yesterday: *with Tactics Logic.* Until now, Nelson hadn't grasped their full implication.

He had a pretty good idea what had become of his two missing pursuers.

* * *

He hadn't bled out. His fractured armor had caught the bullet. What he'd taken for blood had been the spilled contents of the ruptured hydration vest. He was getting some feeling back in his arm and shoulder by the time he came staggering down toward the outer perimeter wire of Firebase Tango, well beyond any reasonable definition of exhaustion. Men were running out to meet him.

The first to arrive was another lean, hard soldier; a three-striper, cast in the same mold as Nelson, but black instead of white. He gave Nelson an appraising look, seemed to see nothing that alarmed him, and flashed his teeth in a grin. "You look like you came through a shit-storm, troop."

"That's about it," said Nelson. "Six dead on the back of the mountain. Yesterday afternoon. An IED." The sergeant was watching him closely, the smile fading. Suddenly the world tilted and spun, taking a full turn, and Nelson's final moments with the Falcon Man flashed back into his mind with hallucinatory clarity.

Only the two of them had been alive at the end—Nelson on his feet, and the bruised and bleeding Falcon Man on the ground, with one arm shattered. Their eyes had met over the point of Nelson's pulse weapon.

Time had slowed. A question had hung in the air. Even now, Nelson wasn't entirely certain what that question had been, or who had asked it. But he had lowered the weapon and thrown down a canteen he'd filled the evening before in the gully. Then he had simply turned and walked away.

Nelson realized that he was sitting on the ground. He was a short way outside of Firebase Tango. His legs had gone. The sergeant was hunkered down beside him, a hand on his shoulder, doing a poor job now of hiding his concern. He motioned to the two soldiers who were running up with a stretcher. The three gently helped Nelson onto it.

"Yeah," said the sergeant. "It's one hell of a war."

At that point BD wobbled by, covered with dust, streaked with hydraulic fluid, dragging the cargo tarp along behind like a tattered cape. The machine was making a line for a break in the wire. BD-428 was completing its mission.

"Looks like you've got yourself a broken dog there," the sergeant commented. It was the sort of thing someone says to distract, to change the subject.

Nelson was up on his elbow, watching BD-428 plod through the gate ahead of them, servo rattling. He watched until BD had disappeared, and then glanced up at the man beside him.

"That's one of the new 400 models," he said to the sergeant. "*That*, my man, is a *Battle Dog*."

蟬

THE JADE CICADA

The logical place to begin, I suppose, is with Chicago, and the events of a particular summer afternoon.

I was in Chinatown, where I'd met a colleague from the university for lunch. We'd had Mongolian hot pot and a couple of cold bottles of Chinese beer, parted company at the end of an hour or so, and I'd wandered off alone into the market, enjoying the pleasant breeze, the bustle of activity, and the scents and colors and sounds. After a while, for no particular reason, I'd turned up a narrow alley and had come out a block or two farther on, onto a quiet and unfamiliar side street. It was there that I'd seen the antique shop.

The bell over the door jingled; a moment passed and an old Chinese gentleman appeared, blinking at me like an owl over a pair of wire-rimmed spectacles. He wore an over-size black cardigan over a neatly pressed white shirt. In one hand was a Chinese newspaper.

"Hi," I said. "Okay if I look around?"

The old man shrugged, leaving me uncertain if he'd actually understood what I said. He took a perch on a stool behind the display case, spreading his newspaper out over the top.

The collection was a good one—certainly much better than I might have expected, judging from the store's location and its air of casual neglect. There were cloisonné vases, very finely worked; a set of old mahjongg tiles, their yellowed ivory polished by many years of frequent handling; there were painted scrolls and some fine porcelain objects as well. Prices were high—as I was beginning to suspect they should be. It was then that I saw the little carving.

"Ah . . ."

I looked up at the sound of the old man's voice.

"Mutton fat jade," he said. "Very nice! Would you care to see?" He came down the back of the display case, taking a key ring from his sweater pocket. For a moment he studied an odd assortment of keys, then the lock turned, the glass slid, and he took out the carved bit of jade.

"A cicada," he announced, gently placing it into my hand. I stroked the surface of the jade with my thumb, immediately liking it. "Do you know what this is?" he asked.

I nodded. "I'm an entomologist." The old man raised his eyebrows. "A person who studies insects," I explained. "My profession."

"Ah, I see. But that is not what I meant. Do you know what *this jade cicada* is?"

The little carving was off-white, lustrous, and slightly translucent, with barely detectable veining. In both color and form it actually looked much like a newly emerged cicada. The workmanship was actually quite wonderful.

"No," I said. "I suppose I don't."

"A grave offering," he said. "A *burial* object." I must have showed some reaction to that, because he quickly shook his head. "This one, I am quite sure, is only a replica. To have happened on an original would be most unusual. *This* one—do you see here?—has a hole drilled through, from one side to the other. So that it can be worn on a cord."

I examined it from the side. Something about the skillful piercing suggested that it hadn't been accomplished using a modern tool. "Why would a cicada be used as a burial object?"

"A very old custom," the old man replied. "Not something done today. But you—an *entomologist*—would surely know about the cicada: How they go into the earth, and come back from the earth. How they break free of the old body, leave it as an empty shell, and then fly up toward the heavens." He gestured vaguely upward. "So . . . the cicada is a *symbol*."

"Of transformation," I said. "Of resurrection . . ."

"Just so! In China, long ago, a jade cicada would be placed into the mouth of one who had died, before that person was buried. As a symbol of that hope, you see. And perhaps for an extra bit of magic? A little magic is a good thing to have in times of trouble."

I smiled. "I suppose it never hurts." I glanced up at him. "How much is it? It doesn't seem to have a price tag."

"As I said, this one is likely a replica. But—as I am sure you will agree—an uncommonly fine one! The jade is of a very high quality. No crack, no flaw . . . I might hope to someday get one hundred dollars for it."

"You might get fifty dollars today . . ."

The old man raised his eyebrows slightly.

"Or maybe even seventy-five," I suggested.

55

He considered for a moment, and then smiled. "I think perhaps that would make us both sufficiently happy." He took the jade cicada from my hand. "It is for you, or for another?"

"A gift," I said. "I'm visiting an old friend that I haven't seen for a while. She's also an entomologist."

"Then I will give you a box, and a velvet bag, and a silk cord to string it on," the old man said. "I'm very sure your friend will like it."

* * *

The jade cicada was to be a gift for Dr. Catherine Montgomery, who had held a special place in my life for a very long time. Our professional relationship was well known—not only at the university, but among a wider circle of entomologists who follow the journals relating to our particular field of study. Our names have often appeared together over the years; I've often cited Catherine's research in my own publications.

Dr. Montgomery had been head of the department when I'd arrived at the university as a graduate student some thirty years ago. She had made quite an impression on me then, and my interest had not been entirely academic. Catherine had been striking. Had there not been an absurd twenty-three years between us—a fact that she had gently pointed out one evening with her characteristic tact and kindness—I suppose things might have been different. As it was, Catherine had become my academic advisor, my mentor, and eventually one of my closest friends.

Catherine had retired almost fifteen years ago, abandoning her Chicago apartment for a farmhouse in southern Indiana. Her departure had closely coincided with my own. I'd left to marry and to take a position at another university.

Years later I'd found myself back in Chicago, taking on my duties as the new head of our old department. The chance to return had come at an opportune moment: A marriage that I'd somehow thought of as happy had recently crashed and burned, the wreckage was still smoldering, and I was in desperate need of a change of scenery. Catherine had won a great deal of respect and admiration during her many years at the university. While my own professional credentials were decidedly sound, I've always suspected that it might have been her personal recommendation that tilted things in my favor.

Catherine and I had kept in touch over the years since. There had been frequent e-mails, regular telephone calls—even occasional meetings, whenever we happened to attend the same professional conferences. Catherine had continued her research after her retirement, but in recent years I couldn't help but notice that she was slowing down. It made me sad to think that time was finally catching up with her.

The object of Catherine's passion had long been the family *Cicadidae*—particularly the genus *Magicicada*, which includes our periodic visitors, the thirteen-year and seventeen-year cicadas. I suppose that will explain why my intended gift seemed so appropriate, and why I'd been so pleased at the serendipity of finding it. Looking back, though, I can see that darker currents had begun stirring at about that time.

You probably know how it is, when you've heard just enough to suspect that there may be bad news ahead, but not quite enough to know with certainty. It was like that, during the weeks leading up to the end of the spring term and my long-delayed visit with Catherine. It all had to do with a few vague hints during the last telephone conversation we'd had.

On some level, I suppose I already knew that Catherine was dying.

* * *

It had been a drive of nearly six hours, from the garage of my north-side condo to the lane leading up to Catherine's farmhouse. Though I'd never before visited there, the turn was easy enough to find; as Catherine had told me, it was directly opposite the gate of an old country cemetery. The cemetery itself was surrounded by a low, wrought iron fence—half-hidden at that point in the season by a profusion of orange lilies—and shaded by an old stand of bur oaks. The sight of the stone markers beyond the fence touched on one of the dark thoughts that had been lurking somewhere just below the surface lately, but I quickly pushed it out of my mind.

My initial impression as I rolled up the drive was that Catherine's home well-suited her. It was a two-story farmhouse, probably built during the first quarter of the previous century. There were tall windows above and below, a porch with turned posts and rail, and lightning rods along the roof ridge, their copper weathered blue-green with the years. Old maples stood sentry at the edges of the yard, providing for areas of sun and shade. Catherine was fond of gardening; where there was sun, there were blooms. Toward the rear of the lot I could see what had probably once been a carriage house. As I got out of my car I heard the sound of a motor from that direction. The scent of newly cut grass hung on the air. Momentarily a man wearing faded bib-overalls came into view, riding on a lawn tractor. I had a glimpse of a perspiring face shaded by the brim of a straw hat before the tractor made a tight turn and disappeared back around the corner.

I climbed the front steps to the porch. There were

wicker chairs and a table, and an old-fashion screen door with turned spindles. The door had the sort of spring I remembered from my childhood—from my grandmother's home in Chicago, where I'd grown up after my parents had died. Such springs made a distinctive sound. This one did too, as the door swung open.

It was not Catherine, but a neatly dressed woman who looked to be well into her sixties. "You're Tom?" she said.

I nodded and took an outstretched hand. There was a faint scent of floral soap about her—something old fashioned; lily-of-the-valley, maybe. "Millie?"

She nodded back, smiling. "We weren't expecting you just yet. Catherine has been taking a nap, but I imagine she heard your car." She held the screen door open for me.

We were in an entry hall, with a staircase opposite the front door. To the left the hall opened onto a sunny, high-ceilinged room, with a polished oak floor and impressively crafted woodwork. I saw leather chairs and an oriental carpet that I remembered from Catherine's apartment in Chicago.

"Like some lemonade?" Millie asked. "I just took a glass out to Mr. Bailey. It's a warm day to be mowing."

She led the way off to the right, through a dining room and into the kitchen, as I tuned my ear to the softer and slower notes of southern Indiana speech. She took a pitcher from the refrigerator, glasses from a cabinet, and we sat down at a kitchen table.

"Sweet enough?"

"It's good," I said. It was.

There was some polite small talk—about the weather and my drive down from Chicago and whether I'd had any trouble finding the house—and then the conversation turned.

"Catherine tells me you two go back a ways," Millie said. "You haven't seen her for a while, though . . ."

"Nearly a year," I admitted. "I guess the last time would have been at the convention in Boston."

"I don't know what all she might have told you," Millie said. "Things aren't so good, Tom. And she's been working too hard. Because . . . Well, time is getting short, I think." She paused for a moment, letting that sink in. "Maybe you can talk some sense into her. Lord knows, *I* haven't been able to." She got up and fetched a couple of coasters for our glasses. I guess she needed something to do to regain her composure. She managed a weak smile as she sat back down. "I suppose you know Catherine well enough. She can be a very stubborn woman sometimes."

It had gotten quiet, and the moment was stretching out. Somewhere beyond the door to the kitchen I could hear a clock slowly ticking.

"What's wrong with her?" I asked. "She . . . hasn't really told me anything specific."

"Oh, it's her heart," Millie said, very matter-of-factly. "There's been a problem for quite a while now. But things have gotten worse lately."

"She's seeing someone, of course . . ."

"She's sensible enough about that, at least. It's just that there's not much to be done."

So, there it was—not at all unexpected, perhaps, but now undeniably real. Until that moment I guess I had managed to convince myself on some level that it might not be.

Millie briefly touched my hand. "I'm sorry, Tom. But you needed to know."

Millie looked up at a sound from the other room, glanced back toward me, and smiled. She raised her voice a little. "Catherine? Your company is here."

I got to my feet as Catherine entered, surprised to find that my legs felt a little unsteady. It quickly passed. I don't think it showed. If I'd expected some outward sign of illness, there wasn't any. There was just Catherine, looking very much as she had the last time I had seen her.

* * *

Catherine and I were sitting outside on the porch after a late dinner, finishing up a bottle of wine. It was a pleasant night, with a newly risen moon low in the east. Inside the house I could hear Millie, humming to herself, washing up the dishes, putting away the silver. The surrounding darkness was alive with the chirping of crickets and the peeping of frogs—certainly not the night sounds I was accustomed to. Briefly, from somewhere around toward the side of the house, came the buzzing drone of an annual cicada.

"His timing is certainly off," Catherine commented. I saw her hand move in the half-light to the jade cicada, which now hung around her neck.

"Do you like it?" I asked.

I couldn't see the smile in the dim light, but I knew it was there. "Very much," she said. "This little fellow is my totem animal, isn't he? I'll never take him off."

Her wicker chair creaked faintly as she picked her glass up from the table. "It would probably seem odd to anyone outside our field that someone's entire life should have revolved around the mysteries of an insect."

"It shouldn't," I said. "Mystery is what life is all about, isn't it?" I sipped my wine, enjoying the way its scent combined with that of the night air. "So . . . How's the research coming?"

"Well enough," Catherine said. "But I suppose I won't be

61

reaching any final answer. Just a final conclusion." She paused. "I assume you had some time to talk with Millie earlier . . ."

This was the difficult part: mutual acknowledgement of what I most dreaded, and what I still wanted to deny.

"We talked," I said.

"That's good. Then we really don't need to worry any more about it, do we?" I knew she was watching me from the shadows. "I want to enjoy this week, Tom. I want your visit to be the only thing special about it. And when it's time for you to go, I want for us to part as we've always done: a little sad, but looking forward to the next time we meet. Agreed?"

"Agreed," I said.

A light came on in a second floor window of the old carriage house at the back of Catherine's property. The upstairs, I'd learned earlier, had been converted into an apartment. It was there that the Baileys were living. Millie was a retired teacher; her husband, Ted, had been a farmer. Now Ted was a part-time handyman. He kept a workshop on the lower level of the old outbuilding, where he "fixed whatever needed fixing".

It seemed to me like a good time to change the subject. The natural topic to turn to was the work we shared:

"Do you think you're any closer to figuring out your cicada clockwork?"

This was the central issue of Catherine's research: the timing mechanism that synchronized the emergence of periodic cicadas. How could billions of insects that lived continuously underground for thirteen or seventeen years—spread out over the broad region claimed by all members of their respective brood—manage to pop out of the earth within a few short days of one another?

"Actually, I'm damn close," she said. "We already know that all cicadas—both annuals and periodicals—share a common emergence trigger, right?"

"Sure," I said. "It's common knowledge: optimal soil temperature."

"So, the periodicals have a secondary mechanism. An *inhibitory* mechanism, which overrides the common trigger. Something that keeps count of the years. Once the requisite number has been reached, it switches off. The periodical reverts to an annual."

"It's a good, common sense theory," I said. "I've always thought so. *Provided*, of course, that you can find your hypothetical inhibitor. It would have to be a molecule that can count."

"Skeptic. Some molecules *do* count." It was a familiar exchange between us. "I think we've almost got it," she said.

"Still running your bugs through a blender?"

She laughed. "Somebody else runs the blender these days. But we've narrowed it down to a couple of remaining molecules. Next summer—year seventeen—should be the one that resolves the whole thing, once and for all. I'd rather hoped to be here for it, but I don't suppose now that I will be."

I'd always known why Catherine had moved to southern Indiana after her retirement. Brood Ten—the seventeen-year cicadas that inhabit the area—had long been the test population for her research. While the magnitude of Brood Ten emergences varied, it was predictably the most numerous and widest spread of any of the seventeen numbered seventeen-year broods. Distribution maps going back as far as 1902 placed Catherine's house somewhere near the historical epicenters.

"There's something I want to ask you to do for me,"

63

Catherine said. "I've hesitated, because I know you'll feel as though you can't refuse . . ."

I interrupted then. I suppose when two people have worked together as closely as we had, they sometimes anticipate one another's thoughts. I was thankful for the shadows. "You don't have to ask," I said. "I'll be here. I'll collect the specimens myself. If we're not both here to do it."

* * *

But we both would not be—as, I suppose, we both had known. It was late that fall when the telephone call from Millie Bailey had come.

The drive back to southern Indiana was the longest and the loneliest I've ever made. I slept in the same upstairs bedroom I'd occupied during the week I'd spent with Catherine only a few months earlier. I was surprised at how many people attended the funeral, although I probably shouldn't have been. I was surprised at how far some of them had come, at how many of them I knew, at how many of those I didn't know seemed to know of me.

I can't really explain how it felt to see Catherine there for the final time. It was Catherine, but it was not. Strung around her neck, over her heart, was the jade cicada I had given her the summer before. I found myself momentarily incapable of speech, disoriented, a bit dizzy. Millie was suddenly standing beside me, holding me by the elbow, telling me quietly that Catherine had requested this sometime after I had left—that she had reminded her again sometime later—that it had seemed very important to Catherine that the cicada should remain with her.

Afterward, much of the funeral was a blur in my mind. At some point I'd been with Millie, watching as the casket was closed and the locks were secured. The procession had backtracked along the same route the Baileys and I had followed earlier that day from Catherine's farmhouse to the funeral home in town. At the end of Catherine's driveway, though, we turned right instead of left, passing through the gateway into the old country cemetery across the road.

The wild orange lilies were gone by then; the acorns had long since fallen from the bur oaks to the ground; far across the road, in Catherine's yard, the blooms of the previous summer had vanished. Now there were the colors of fall. The leaves of the tall maples in her yard had turned a bright yellow.

It was a clear October afternoon. Insects were singing in the grass and the fields, but all of the annual cicadas had fallen silent many weeks before, when Catherine had no doubt been there to bid them a final farewell. On the trunks of the oaks only a few of their empty husks remained, cast off on a past summer night, of no further use.

I was a pall bearer. I remained behind with Millie after most of the others had left, to see the casket lowered into the ground and to throw a handful of earth into the grave. Afterward, Ted Bailey took my car on ahead as Millie and I walked slowly back to Catherine's house. The house, too, seemed to me like an empty husk. Millie and I sat on the porch for a while before going inside. Somehow I didn't want to. That which had previously filled the house with life had gone away.

Following Catherine's funeral I remained on for a week. Most of that time I spent collecting together Catherine's research data, which was already surprisingly well organized; I suspect she had seen to that with the intention of making things easier for me. Midweek I received a call requesting my presence at the office of Catherine's attorney. When I arrived there on the following afternoon, I realized that I had previously met him at the funeral. He was an affable fellow—a small-town lawyer who had a way of putting one at ease with the prospect of unavoidable legal formalities. I was surprised when he informed me that Catherine had willed me her home and most of its contents. I had also been left a sum of money, with a smaller but by no means insignificant amount going to Mr. and Mrs. Bailey.

What was I to do with Catherine's home? That was a question I was totally incapable of resolving, and would likely have trouble thinking about for some time. In any event, I had made a promise; I would be returning to southern Indiana again during the following spring, and remaining there until my promise had been kept. Probably by then I'd be able to think things through and be able to decide. In the meantime, Millie and Ted were pleased with my request that they remain on in my absence. They would stay in their apartment and tend to the upkeep of the house and grounds until my return. I drove back to Chicago satisfied with the arrangements, and took some small comfort from the thought that Catherine likely would have been satisfied as well.

* * *

The seasons passed quickly, as they always do; fall gave way to a cold and dreary Chicago winter; spring term began; February, March, and April came and went, and I soon found myself clearing my schedule for a return to southern Indiana.

My thoughts had never been far from Catherine during the time since I had left. It could hardly have been otherwise: I spent my days in a place where we had long worked together, surrounded by people we both had known; I passed my evenings at home studying the notes and data that represented thirty years of Catherine's work, following her thoughts until I came to the place where she had stood the summer before, on the verge of an answer to the question that had so occupied her. By then the question had come to fascinate me as it had fascinated her.

I'd have to admit that there was another dimension to the depth of my involvement—something beyond a simple matter of professional interest or scientific curiosity. I suppose what had happened was that I had submerged much of the pain of the loss in my own ongoing pursuit of Catherine's goal. So long as I was following after her, it seemed that Catherine was somehow still near, looking over my shoulder. I sometimes wondered if that sense of continuing closeness might not be a symptom of denial—if, perhaps, I was not coming to terms with the finality of Catherine's death as I really should. Death, after all, is the ultimate finality—and one that I didn't seem to be allowing myself to openly confront.

I wasn't at all certain what would happen when the work finally ended, when my promise to Catherine had been kept, when I would have to leave Catherine and my source of comfort behind. It was another question that I was always quick to push from my thoughts. So, when summer came, I carried it with me back to Catherine's former home, like a bit of unnoticed baggage. Or maybe—in retrospect—like an unexploded bomb.

* * *

I had gotten a much later start than I'd intended, and called Millie midway through the drive to let her know I was running late. By the time I turned up the lane toward the farmhouse the sun was rapidly dropping below the horizon. Beneath the cover of the spreading oaks across the road, the cemetery was already hidden in deepening shadows.

Happily, Millie had turned on the lights in Catherine's

house, so I wasn't met with the forlorn sight of dark windows that I'd half expected. After we had exchanged greetings beneath the porch light, I discovered that her efforts had gone far beyond that: The dining room table was set; a pot roast was waiting; the scents from the kitchen were delightful. I suddenly realized that I hadn't eaten since breakfast and that breakfast had been a very long time before. I took my meal that first evening with the Baileys, grateful not to be eating alone.

Afterward, as Millie cleared the table, Ted helped me move my luggage from the trunk of my car upstairs to the guest bedroom. Only sometime later—after the Baileys had bid me a good night and retreated to their apartment—did it occur to me that *they* had actually been the guests; I would be sleeping in a house that now belonged not to Catherine, but to me.

Sometime during that first night I had a very peculiar dream. The dream featured Catherine—Catherine as she had been many years ago—and the old Chinese gentleman from the antique shop.

In the dream, the two were talking to one another with quiet, focused attention. I suddenly realized that I couldn't understand what they were saying; that they were speaking in what sounded to me like some sort of Chinese dialect. I seemed to be only a fly on the wall—a disembodied presence, whose only role was that of an observer. Then Catherine turned, smiling, and looked directly into my eyes.

I was startled awake. The details of the dream fled as I realized where I was.

As I slept the moon had risen. Pale moonlight was streaming in through the bedroom window, falling across the interior of the room, over the covers of the bed. I'd left the window up, and the lace curtains were stirring in the cool night breeze. As I watched the play of light and shadow, the breeze freshened and curtains billowed; the bedroom door, which I had left ajar for better ventilation, moved slightly, and I caught the motion of it from the corner of my eye. As I turned to look, somewhere beyond the door a floorboard out in the hallway creaked.

My heart skipped a beat.

The sound had been faint, but it was one that I remembered from my first visit the summer before.

For a moment I lay completely still, listening, hardly breathing, trying to calm myself. There were only the sounds of chirping crickets and night peepers outside in the darkness. I fumbled for the switch on the bedside lamp, hitting the shade, nearly knocking the whole thing over. Rationality returned with the light of a twenty-five watt bulb.

I felt foolish.

On the nightstand, beneath the lamp, was the paperback book I'd been reading a couple of hours earlier. I considered reading another page or two, but thought better of it when I noticed that the clock on the nightstand showed the time to be nearly a quarter after three.

I realized that my throat was dry. Probably I wouldn't fall sleep again until I'd had some water. Reluctantly I got out of bed and went out into the hallway.

I couldn't remember where the wall switch was. The light from my room was barely enough to make out the top of the stairs to my right, and the receding shapes of the doorways that lined either side of the hall. The door to the bath was midway down. The vague dark patch at the far end was the door to the master bedroom—the room that had been Catherine's.

I felt my way along the hall.

The sudden brightness of the bathroom fixture was dazzling. After drying my hands and glancing at myself in the mirror, I switched off the light.

The hallway was even darker now than before. I stood in the gloom, letting my eyes adjust.

It suddenly occurred to me that I hadn't looked into the master bedroom since I'd been back. The idea made me unaccountably uneasy. I suppose that's why I decided that I should do so.

I approached through the darkness, took hold of the knob—and hesitated.

The dream had come back to me.

What I did next was irrational: I knocked—very softly, as if not wanting to awaken someone who might be sleeping—and waited.

The absurdity of the situation hit me.

I turned the knob and pushed, but the door was unyielding.

It seemed to be locked.

* * *

Millie had gotten up early, let herself in, and was setting a plate and silverware out on the table when I came into the dining room.

"Did you sleep well?" she said.

I sat down heavily. "Not really."

"Probably it's too quiet for you. Chicago, right? Cities are never really quiet." She placed a mug of coffee in front of me, disappeared back into the kitchen, and returned with sausages and eggs. "You'll get use to it."

"I didn't know breakfasts were part of the arrangement."

"They're not," she said. She fetched her own cup and sat down across from me. "It's just that you still seem like company."

"Huh. Here I was thinking of myself as Lord of the Manor." I dove into the eggs and sausages. "Maybe we could negotiate? About dinners, I mean. I'm OK when it comes to breakfast and lunch, but by the end of the day I get tired of my own cooking."

"We could do that," Millie said. "You could buy the groceries. I could cook, and the three of us could take our evening meals together. How would that be?"

"Sounds good," I replied. "I'll have my lawyer call your lawyer."

She smiled. "Around here, everybody's got the same lawyer."

"Ah. Then we've met. I assume he comes to dinner, too?"

"He's been known to."

Millie became thoughtful. "You know, Tom—Ted and I had no idea that Catherine was going to leave us anything. It made us both feel a little . . . odd, somehow. She was much more of a friend than an employer."

"Sure," I said. "I know that. I'm sure that's exactly why she did it."

She studied her coffee for a moment before she spoke again. "You'll be working here through the summer? Finishing up what Catherine was doing?"

"I hope so," I said. "To find what she was looking for, I mean. I'll definitely be staying to collect the specimens. That will be done by June. After that, there will be lab work—somebody else does that—and then an analysis of the data. I may write a paper summarizing the results later on."

"I suppose you'll be doing that part back in Chicago."

I nodded.

"Will you be selling the house?"

71

"Probably," I said. "To tell the truth, I've been having trouble thinking about that."

"I suspected you might be," she said. "Since we're telling truths, I'll tell *you* one: I was happy not to leave right after Catherine died." She looked out through the dining room window. "Sometimes it almost seems like she's still around here. Out in the garden, or somewhere around the house. Sometimes I've felt that very strongly." She looked back to me. "But I'm alright about going, now. Time has sort of gotten me used to the idea. Ted and I have our own house in town. You knew that, didn't you?"

"Actually, I didn't."

"Sure. We're just fine. We can stay on here and take care of the place for as long as you want—but we're fine, whenever it's time to go."

"I'll let you know what's going on, as soon as I figure it out for myself."

I finished my breakfast; we both finished our coffee; Millie began clearing up the table.

"By the way," I said, "do you know where the key to the upstairs bedroom is?"

She came back from the kitchen. "The guest bedroom, you mean? Where you're staying?"

"No, the master bedroom. Catherine's old room."

"I'm not even sure there is a key." She gave me a puzzled look. "Why?"

"I think the door's locked," I said.

She shook her head. "The door has never been locked. I haven't been in there for a while. Not since we cleared out Catherine's closets. We packed up most of her clothing and took it over to the church after she died," she said. "She asked me to do that. So you wouldn't have to be bothered with it."

"Ah."

"Probably the door is just sticking," she said. "Ted fixed that for her a couple of times. It's an old house. Things get out of alignment, and the wood swells this time of year. Just try giving the door a good shove."

Millie was right, of course. I tried the door again after breakfast. The night before, it had only been sticking. With a turn of the knob and a bit of a push it easily came open.

There was only a bedroom: a queen-size bed, neatly made up; a nightstand with a lamp; a mirrored dresser; empty closets.

I don't know what else I might have expected.

* * *

As the days passed—as I waited for the last week of May and the coming of the cicadas—I quickly fell into a morning routine. I rose early and had a cup of coffee; afterward, I walked to the edge of town and back, a round-trip of a bit over five miles.

I had long been in the habit of morning walks along the Chicago lakefront, but here it wasn't only about getting my exercise. I was observing the local surroundings, trying to determine the best places to collect my cicada specimens when the time came. Careful planning was essential. While the Brood Ten emergence would stretch out over several days, the optimal time for collection would be brief.

Cicada nymphs emerge from the soil during the night— the majority of them during the course of the same one or two nights. They climb a few feet up the nearest vertical surface—usually the trunk of the tree they've been feeding on over the years—and by the following morning will have wriggled free of their shells, darkened from white to black, deployed their transparent wings, and taken to the air. I would have to collect a thousand or more shortly after they

73

emerged from the soil, still in their shells. Catching them at that point was essential. There was uncertainty about the persistence of the presumed timing molecule subsequent to emergence and the final stage of metamorphosis.

After a few days, I decided that the old graveyard across the road would probably be the ideal location. It was convenient to the house; the grounds hadn't been subjected to chemical lawn treatments or agricultural chemicals, and there were a great many mature trees. I had seen the cast-off shells of annual cicadas still clinging to the trunks of the massive bur oaks during the past fall. Where conditions were good for annuals, they would almost certainly be right for their seventeen-year cousins. Catherine had very likely intended to collect specimens there herself.

I had already inspected Catherine's work area—a room just off the garage on the ground floor of the carriage house. There I'd found a dozen cylindrical collection cages. She had made them of rolled rabbit wire and strapped them together in pairs; each pair was fitted with a shoulder strap, so that four could be easily carried at a time.

There was also a horizontal freezer. I'd lifted the lid and discovered it would accommodate all twelve of the collection cages. The freezer could be used to dispatch the captured insects; brief exposure to sub-zero temperatures would do the job quickly and humanely, and hold no risk of skewing the results of subsequent chemical analysis. I'd checked the plug, turned the dial all the way down, and was gratified to hear the compressor motor kick in.

Beside the freezer I'd found a dozen corrugated boxes, each with a Styrofoam cooler that fit neatly inside. The boxes already had overnight shipping labels with a number to call for pick-up. I would only have to make a trip to town to find some dry ice. A note taped to one of the coolers told me where I could do that.

Catherine had been nothing if not thorough.

* * *

On the morning of May 19, I saw the first cast-off cicada shell on the trunk of an oak at the center of the old cemetery. I was fairly certain that it was a periodical, not an annual. Early the next morning I counted six. By mid-afternoon the day was warm and the sky clear.

While I suspected the main emergence wouldn't come until another full night had passed, I really couldn't be sure. I drove into town for my dry ice and stowed away a plentiful supply in the freezer. I then made several trips down the lane and across the road with the collection cages, which I hid out of sight behind Catherine's headstone.

I set the alarm for 11:30 pm and went to bed an hour after dinner. Just after midnight, I made my way over to the cemetery and inspected the trees by lantern and moonlight. A few more cicadas were slowly climbing tree trunks here and there, but the total count was still very low. I returned to my bed. It took me a long time to fall asleep.

The early morning light woke me up. I dressed and had a coffee. Again I inspected the oaks. Half-a-dozen nymph shells clung to the bark of every tree—the upturn of a bell curve about to go nearly vertical.

Below the turf, beneath the woods beyond the fence, and for a hundred miles in every direction, something was stirring. I had no doubt at all about the coming night.

Brood Ten was awakening.

* * *

There seemed to be little chance of sleep that night. My anticipation was running far too high. Still, I double-checked the alarm. I'd had very little rest the night before and didn't want to miss the appointed hour.

75

G. S. HARGRAVE

I ran through my mental checklist one final time, reassuring myself that all was in order. I then switched off the lamp and lay back on my pillow.

Time passed. I'm not sure how much.

I vaguely recall the curtains stirring in the darkness. I recall feeling a slight chill and realizing that I'd left the windows up. I remember, too, thinking about getting up to close them, but that doing so had seemed like entirely too much trouble.

At some point I drifted off into unconsciousness.

Perhaps you're aware of a phenomenon known as sleep paralysis? It's a perfectly normal condition—a suspension of voluntary motor functions that routinely occurs during certain phases of sleep. It's what keeps us from doing damage, while we're in the grip of those nightly hallucinations commonly known as dreams. Most often we're unconscious of the condition, because most often we're unconscious when we're in it. Once in a while, though, things can get a little mixed up.

It might have gone differently, if I'd had some previous experience with this.

I was aware that I was on a bed, that the bed was in a room, that the room was upstairs in Catherine's house; so far, so good. When I tried to move, though, *absolutely nothing happened.*

I suppose fear might be a common reaction. It certainly was mine.

A series of increasingly disturbing possibilities flew though my mind in rapid succession. They came faster and faster until I hit on the most frightening possibility of all, like a bird smacking head on into a plate glass window:

Perhaps I was dead.

It took a breathless minute for reason—or at least

something approximating it—to return.

That's completely irrational, I thought. *If I were dead, I wouldn't be wondering about it.*

I took a quick inventory of myself: There was no pain; I was breathing; my heart was beating . . .

Whatever the hell I was, it certainly wasn't dead.

It was *Catherine* who was . . .

I recoiled, horrified, but too late. The thought had me. It took possession of my imagination, and my imagination transmuted it into visions.

Images tumbled through my brain with the furious intensity of fever delirium: Catherine, in her casket; the casket, beneath the ground; the depredations of water, mold, and worm . . . All of it was welling up unchecked out of some primordial darkness into the interior of my skull, which was rapidly filling with terror and madness—flooding, like the hold of a doomed ship.

One needed magic—or an ally—to fend off such a terrifying attack. Throughout my life—since the childhood death of my parents—I had been a creature of logic; consequently, I had neither.

There was a *crack!* and a flash and an electrical jolt. If my brain had a fuse, it had apparently just popped.

The terrors were retreating—slowly at first, and then more quickly—like water gaining momentum as it spiraled and then rushed away down a pipe. In its place, the room was emerging from the darkness—the dim shapes of familiar objects—windows, walls, furnishings, curtains.

The scene pulled into sharper focus. It was not quite right. All around me was motionless, yet everything—every shape and shadow—was moving, pulsating with restless energy, as though the room itself had come to life.

I was still on the bed; simultaneously, I was not: I also

77

seemed to be standing beside it, in a room superimposed over a room.

I was disembodied. I was quite literally beside myself, gazing down on my own sleeping form.

It was at that point that I ceased to analyze. Analysis had become utterly pointless.

Apparently it is possible to be not only disembodied, but a disembodied sleepwalker. I was moving out of the bedroom and into the hallway. I lingered there, acutely conscious of the door at the far end of the hall. That, however, was apparently not where I was meant to go. Instead, I found myself descending the staircase.

I was in the entry hall. I could hear the slow ticking of the clock. The front door stood open; the screen door had swung wide. I crossed the porch, descended the steps, and went out onto the lawn. The grass was damp with dew, cold beneath my bare feet.

Suddenly I knew my destination.

I entered the cemetery through the open gate. The moon was full and bright, looking down on the world through a near-transparent veil of fleeting clouds. By its light the wrought iron fence cast its shape onto the lawn. The trunks of the oaks rose up from the earth to be lost in the shadows above, like massive, gnarly columns supporting an unseen vault.

On every trunk there was movement.

I crossed to the nearest tree and dropped to my knees; I inspected the soil around its base. Cicada nymphs were emerging. They were wriggling up out of the earth everywhere. My eyes followed the wave of movement upward. The trunk was already covered with a climbing mass of insects as far up as I could see, and no doubt above that. Here and there some had already cast off their exoskeletal shells, while others were in the process of doing so. Those already broken free shone white and pale—eerie shapes of luminosity in the moonlight.

I had gone over all of this in my mind a hundred times before in preparation for the night; I suppose it was only natural that my actions should have become automatic.

I got to my feet and made my way across the cemetery, passing between headstones toward the place where I had left the collection cages. The strangeness of all that had happened before was momentarily forgotten—I was even annoyed with myself for having neglected to bring my lantern. Then I realized that I had come to the foot of Catherine's grave.

Beneath the grass, in the dark recesses below, I knew that something was stirring.

I backed away one step, and then another, and collided with an unseen headstone. My eyes were fixed on the patch of earth before me.

Pale light and shadow were rippling across the surface.

From all around—from the cemetery, from the shadows of surrounding woods—there came a faint, oscillating hum.

It was too early—on the first night, by the cold light of the moon—but I recognized the sound immediately. It was the chorusing of cicadas.

The rippling light on the grave began to swirl, a whirlpool running backward, the tempo and brightness increasing with the rising hum. The hum became a throbbing vibration, a howling roar, as the shining vortex pulsated, rose above the ground, and suddenly burst upward in a fountain of luminosity.

Standing above the grave was a shining form—a being newly born, just emerged. There were features—a face that I recognized.

Her eyes found mine.

I had been called to witness this, but seeing was more than I could endure.

I fell to my knees as the darkness swirled in around me.

The oscillation retreated, turned inward onto itself, and became the buzzing of the alarm clock on the nightstand beside my bed.

Half-past eleven.

I groped in the dark, this time knocking the lamp off the nightstand. I slapped at the alarm and shut it off. I sat there alone in the darkness—stunned—shaking—sobbing—still unsure what was real.

Slowly it came to me that something had changed.

The unrelenting sorrow—a weight that had pressed down on my heart for so long that I had ceased even to recognize it—had gone. In its place was a forgotten lightness that I hadn't felt since my earliest childhood.

My mind began to work again. All that was left was to keep my promise. That was the thing that I needed to do.

I found my shoes and slipped them on. I went down the staircase for what seemed like a second time. On the stand by the door was the lantern. This time I didn't forget it.

I gathered up the collection cages from where I'd left them. It felt right that I had left them near Catherine's grave.

During the hours that followed, by moonlight and lantern, I collected our cicada nymphs. By mid-morning they all had been packed into their shipping cartons and were on their way to the lab.

* * *

I suppose I should tie up a few loose ends before I bring this to a close.

Analysis of the specimens bore out Catherine's

hypothesis concerning a specific timing molecule present in the Brood Ten cicadas. The molecule has an inhibitory function, exactly as she thought: It keeps count of the passage of the years by way of an incremental lengthening of the molecular chain, and ceases to inhibit once it has reached a requisite length.

I published the results the following year in Catherine's name, taking a co-author credit so that our names might appear together one final time. I'm pleased to say that the paper generated considerable interest within our little world of beetles and bugs. New studies are likely, to extend the results to the remaining broods of seventeen-year cicadas. No doubt the thirteen-year varieties will receive attention as well.

I sold Catherine's house. I kept a few mementos, of course: The big oriental carpet is now in my Chicago apartment, along with a bookcase, a leather sofa, a couple of favorite old chairs, and quite a few volumes from Catherine's library. Millie and Ted took their pick of what remained before I auctioned off what was left.

There's one remaining matter, and I have debated with myself what I should say about it. I know that it's very important. It was, after all, the thing that precipitated a sort of paradigm shift in my own personal cosmology. But it also seems very private. I suppose I also realize that it will stretch my credibility to the breaking point.

I will be circumspect. You can take my words for whatever you think they're worth.

It has to do with what I found on the nightstand beside Catherine's bed, when I looked into her room the morning after the cicada emergence.

I'm wearing it beneath my shirt, for a little extra magic.

I'll never take it off.

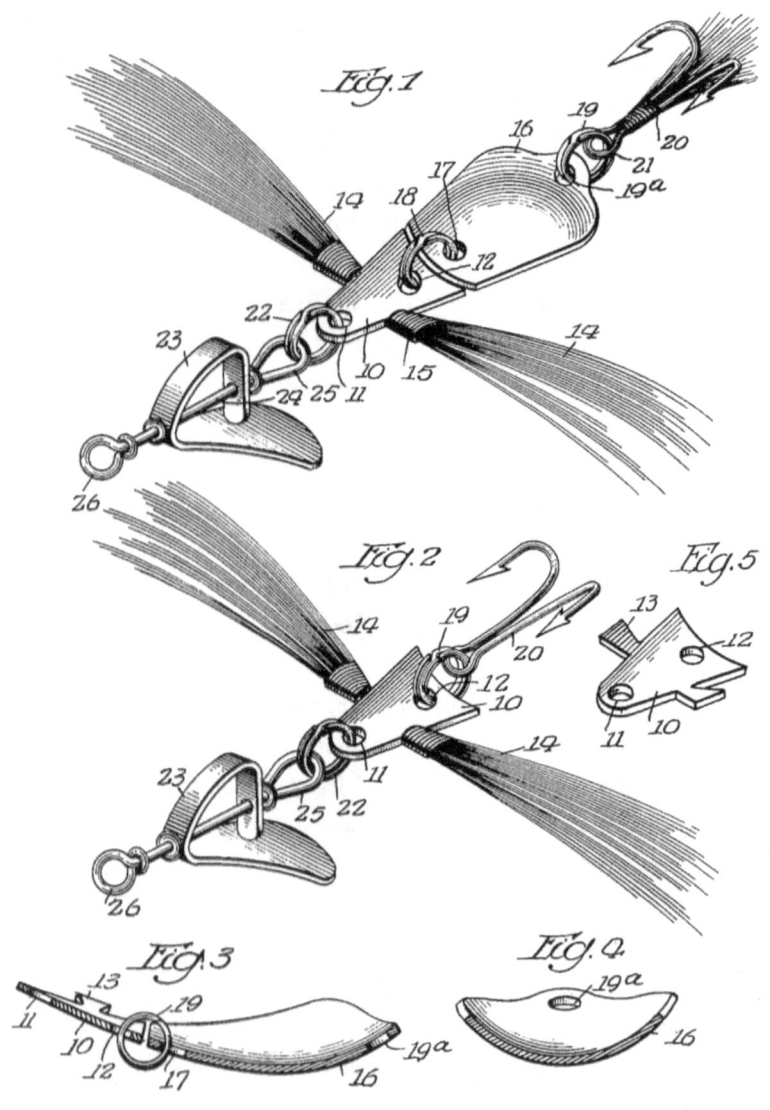

Fig.1

Fig.2

Fig.5

Fig.3

Fig.4

ON SOME BRIGHT STREAM

It had been a perfectly routine morning until the alarms unexpectedly sounded. Cups of coffee were knocked over, assorted pastries were abandoned, and conversations were broken off in mid-sentence as technicians scrambled for their ring of control room monitors, suddenly intent on nothing but getting back to their work stations.

The frantic moment passed quickly. Normalcy was returning in the form of an automatic Large Hadron Collider shutdown by the time the last stragglers had made it back to their chairs.

One hundred meters down, along a vastly larger, steel-incased ring lit with fluorescent tubes, the howling horns fell silent. As the last fading echoes chased themselves in 27-kilometer circles, three physicists in an underground monitoring station a couple of kilometers out failed to notice that the howling had stopped. They were too occupied with their efforts to come to terms with something else.

Normalcy wasn't a word that seemed to have any local application at the moment.

Dr. Hansen, the monitoring station supervisor, was the first to collect his wits. He entered some keystrokes and stared hard at the data display they brought up. What he saw there only deepened his sense of unreality.

Somewhere out along the ring, an impending moment of magnetic instability had been detected by the computers and an automatic shutdown had been initiated. A couple of very specific events should have followed: A four terawatt wallop of stored particle beam energy should have hit the carbon beam dump in a matter of nanoseconds for safe dissipation, and the resultant heat and radiation spikes should now be displaying on Hansen's monitor.

It *hadn't*, and they *weren't*. Apparently a brief energy pulse roughly equivalent to a quarter of all of the electrical power being used on the planet at any given moment had simply vanished down a rabbit hole.

Hansen blinked at his monitor, wondering if he might actually be at home in his Geneva apartment, asleep and dreaming.

Jeffries, his young English colleague, was the first of the three to find some appropriate words: "*What* the bloody hell was *that*?"

No one doubted what it was that Jeffries was referring to: As a few thousand switches had been tripped to their *off* positions with super-human precision, something inside their little monitoring station room had gone decidedly wonky. There had been a dull *pop*, felt as much as heard, and a spherical pattern of diminishing ripples had briefly radiated outward from a point at the room's center. Empty space there had momentarily resembled a liquid mirror that had just swallowed an invisible, dropped pebble.

"Direct neural stimulation," Fritz Lutz said. The bald little German was clearly rattled. "A hallucination, induced by an electromagnetic pulse."

Jeffries responded with a rude noise, tapping his own fully functional computer monitor with a wooden pencil. "You know better, Fritzie. An EMP that strong would have buggered every PC from here to Geneva."

"Well," said Hansen, straightening up his tall frame, "there's *no record* of a pulse. There are no dump spikes, either."

Fritzie quickly brought up the same data display on his own monitor. His eyebrows arched toward the top of his head like a pair of startled black caterpillars. "That much energy doesn't just . . . *evaporate*. There *must* have been an EMP! Part leaked through some localized fault in the shielding." Fritzie's eyes shifted uneasily toward the center of the room. "It missed the computers, but hit a data conduit somewhere. And it hit *us*. What we *thought* we saw was only a neurological event."

"That's bad news for you, Fritzie," said Jeffries. "You already had a couple of blown fuses." Jeffries rocked back in his chair and laced his fingers behind his shaggy blond head. "An EMP that strong would have registered *somewhere*."

Fritzie stared at his screen. "You can think of some *better* explanation?"

"I'm pretty much clueless," Jeffries confessed after a moment. "Maybe there were funny mushrooms on the lunchroom pizza."

Dr. Hansen tapped a couple of keys to save a local copy of the data. Doing so made little sense, of course; the interesting thing about the data set was what was unaccountably *missing* from it. He glanced again toward the center of the room, picking up a stray pen off his monitor desk and unconsciously holding it as he might hold a fly rod. Hansen was an avid fly fisherman. He did some of his best thinking with a fly rod in his hand.

Unless something better came along, he decided, he'd probably have to go along with Fritzie and write the whole thing off as the transient effects of a localized EMP. That seemed plausible, at least.

Besides, what the hell else could it have been?

* * *

Whatever it was, a few days after the collider restart it happened again. Horns blared out another warning along 27 kilometers of imperceptibly curving, fluorescent-lit tunnels. On the surface, more break room coffee was spilled. There was another cascade of swiftly tripping switches, and the same three startled physicists in the same underground monitoring station jumped at the sound of another dull *pop*. For three or four seconds, empty space at the center of the room rippled and pulsed. Afterward, there was another impossible absence of heat and radiation spikes from the carbon beam dump.

It didn't take long for perplexity to spread beyond the confines of one particular monitoring station, nor for rumors of two decidedly odd occurrences there to make the rounds of CERN. Much to Fritzie's annoyance, the monitoring station report was promptly tag lined as *Fritzie's UFO*. With the most ambitious and expensive scientific apparatus ever to have existed on the planet inexplicably malfunctioning, however, talk soon turned serious, and a consensus emerged that Fritzie's explanation was most likely correct: There *had* to have been an EMP, since disruption of the data stream was the only rational explanation for the missing radiation spikes; the bizarre events witnessed in the monitoring room had *surely* been neurological phenomena—an interpretation that only lent greater credibility to the EMP theory.

Fritzie's fur—what little there was of it—might have been smoothed, had Jeffries not stubbornly refused to sign on to the consensus opinion. The young Englishman often took contrary views purely as a matter of principle, Hansen had observed, but in this particular case he suspected something more was afoot than mere predisposition.

Hansen's suspicion was confirmed when Jeffries arrived at the monitoring station one morning with a video camera and tripod, which he proceeded to set up facing the center of the room.

"There's a motion detector," Jeffries said. "I'm leaving it on twenty-four-seven. If the bugger shows up again, *I'm* getting pictures."

Hansen and Fritzie exchanged glances, but neither commented. The theory that they had actually observed two external, recordable events might be on the far side of unlikely, but there was little fault they could find with Jeffries' proposed method for testing it.

Fritzie's generally accepted EMP theory wasn't without its own set of consequences, of course. Apparently some obscure malfunction had twice set loose unexpected, oddly focused electromagnetic pulses that might have produced dangerous local results. The Large Hadron Collider would remain offline until the fault was discovered. Technicians and designers would be crisscrossing the 27-kilometer ring and its attendant chambers and service tunnels for at least a week, checking superconducting magnets, helium cooling systems, power feeds, innumerable sensors, and endless optical and electrical cables, while programmers one hundred meters above tested the collider's controlling software with an exhaustive series of operation simulations.

With the collider unexpectedly down, the monitoring room crew suddenly found themselves at loose ends. Fritzie announced that he was off to Paris to see a woman he'd met at a recent symposium, while Jeffries decided to visit Amsterdam for a couple of days on one of his mysterious excursions. Dr. Hansen predictably loaded his fishing gear into his Audi wagon, which he pointed toward a favorite Swiss village near a favorite river.

Such opportunities didn't come often.

* * *

Switzerland has much to offer the avid fly fisherman. Hansen took a room at an old hotel where he was already known by name, looking forward to spending the next four days in mountain air and summer sunshine, knee-deep in clear cold water.

While Hansen was a passionate fisherman, his passion had little to do with the acquisition of fish. He had rarely kept a catch since his long past Minnesota boyhood. For Hansen, fly fishing was more about the Zen of an empty mind; about harmonizing breath and movement and stillness with the rhythms of the natural world around him. There was a quiet, contemplative joy to be found in gazing across the shining surface of the water, in reading first one subtle sign and then another, and in knowing without thought where his quarry would be as the moment came to cast. There were far worse places to spend one's idle days than on some bright stream.

This wasn't to say that Hansen didn't appreciate a well turned out trout. The charming little restaurant across from his hotel did some memorable things with them. After each day in his waders Hansen took full advantage of that, washing down a predictably splendid meal with a few glasses of his favorite French wine. Catch and release was his sportsman's prerogative, not a moral position.

Each evening, aglow with the food and the wine, Hansen would retire to his cozy little second floor room to listen to a bit of classical music on the radio while inspecting and repairing his hand-tied flies. This was a far more analytical activity than the art of fly fishing itself; it was a matter of applied science, in a way. Fly tying was something that his grandfather had taught him. Lures—as the romantic in Hansen thought of them—were the magical attractors. It was important that they be *just so*. As he lovingly tended to them, he tried to imagine seeing them with the eye of a trout.

* * *

The last glory of a summer day was fading as Hansen reached the entrance to his Geneva apartment building, pleasantly tired from four days on the river. Upstairs, after unpacking and putting away his gear, he made himself a sandwich, twisted the cap off a bottle of beer, and sat down at his computer to log in on his CERN account.

He found the last *LHC Status Report* that he'd read before leaving and worked his way forward. A number of minor problems had been identified and corrected, along with an intermittent synchronization issue in Section 4-5 of the collider ring that was thought to have been a likely cause for the unexpected shutdowns. There were still final tests to be completed, but it was anticipated that the start-up sequence might commence as early as mid-week.

Hoozah, Hansen thought to himself, and saluted the screen with his bottle. It was a decidedly qualified *hoozah*. His enthusiasm would be more serious when anticipation actually gave way to a successful restart. He took a bite from his sandwich and clicked on his e-mail.

There were three messages from Jeffries, with copies to Fritz Lutz. Two had been sent yesterday morning—the day Jeffries had presumably gotten back from Amsterdam: *We need to talk. Please call ASAP. Jeffries*; and then: *Important! Call me as soon as you're in!* The third had been sent late yesterday evening. Hansen frowned. All it said was: *URGENT! Where the bloody hell are you?*

Hansen put down his sandwich and reached for the phone, but both Jeffries' home and cell numbers went unanswered. He left a short voice message on each and typed a reply to the last e-mail for good measure: *Just got in. Called you but no answer. I'll be back at the lab tomorrow morning. Phone me at home if it can't wait. Hansen.* Then he finished his sandwich.

An hour later, as Hansen finally called it a night, no call had come.

* * *

Hansen arrived at the monitoring station a bit after nine o'clock the following morning. Jeffries wasn't there, but was apparently around somewhere; his jacket was draped over the back of his chair and a half-empty cup of tea sat near his keyboard. Hansen noted Jeffries' tripod was still present, minus the video camera.

Fritzie came buzzing in half an hour later. His enthusiastic narration about Paris was decidedly more colorful than Hansen's brief account of his own fishing trip. Fritzie was expecting a call from his "paramour" later that morning. Hansen smiled to himself at the word.

By ten they'd gotten down to business. There were schedules to review and systems checks to run in preparation for Wednesday's expected start-up. It was eleven o'clock before Jeffries' continued absence struck either of them as unusual.

"I wonder where he is," Fritzie said.

"No clue." Hansen glanced at his watch. "I suppose you saw his e-mails . . ."

Fritzie nodded and looked toward Jeffries' work station. "Obviously he's been here."

Hansen considered the coat and cup, for the first time wondering exactly when they might have been left.

He minimized a running sensor check program screen and brought up his CERN e-mail account. There was nothing new from his missing colleague. He checked his voice messages via the land line and drew another blank. Then he dialed Jeffries' home and let it ring for a while. Jeffries' cell number got him a service unavailable message, which might only mean he was underground somewhere in the complex.

Another forty minutes passed.

"This really isn't like him," Fritzie said.

Hansen had just been looking at Jeffries' e-mails again, thinking the same thing. "Maybe I should check at his apartment."

"You have a key?"

"I think I know where one is," Hansen said. "I fed the cat when he was in London for his sister's wedding."

Fritzie glanced toward the empty chair, frowning. "I think maybe you should."

* * *

No one answered Hansen's knock. He found the spare key hidden behind the window box that was planted with pink petunias and let himself in.

The cat was waiting just inside the door, very glad to see him. Hansen picked her up and gave her a scratch behind the ears.

"Jeffries?"

There was no response.

In the kitchen, the cat's dish was empty. Hansen found her kibble, filled the bowl, and set her down beside it. She dove into the food with unusual enthusiasm.

He glanced around the kitchen. Plates, cups, and glasses were in the drainer; a few waited to be washed in the sink. In the bedroom he found the bed unmade, covers roughly drawn up over the pillows. That was about as much attention as he ever gave the matter himself. In the bath a dry towel hung over the shower curtain rod. Everything seemed normal enough.

Hansen reentered the living room. On the floor, unnoticed at first, was Jeffries' video camera. It was jacked into the television.

Hansen idly picked it up and pushed the *play* button. The tiny monitor filled with static. He ran the index back to zero and found himself looking at a still frame of the monitoring room. The time stamp matched the first day that Fritzie, Jeffries, and he had been absent. Hansen sat down on the carpet and turned on the TV.

There were three separate events recorded over as many days, each around 10 seconds in duration.

He'd seen and heard this all before—or something very similar, at least. The same odd *pop*, the same curious spread of ripples in the air.

"Huh," Hansen said to himself. "It was *real*."

Something, though, had seemed a bit different.

He jumped the index back to the beginning. Timing the pause was difficult, but on the third event he got it right. He moved closer to the screen, advancing the image frame by frame. When he found the one he wanted he pushed the *zoom* button, and then hit *play* and *slow.*

At the center of the distortion a small, curiously exotic object suddenly appeared, rotating around a tilted axis. After a second it vanished.

Hansen slowly stood up, caught up in another moment that felt like a dream. He was trying hard to put his thoughts in order.

The two original disturbances had somehow been caused by a collider fault. First one disturbance and then another, each coinciding with a beam dump and absent radiation spikes. He remembered what Fritzie had said on the first occasion: *"That much energy doesn't just evaporate."*

Nor does something just appear out of nowhere, he thought.

Hansen stared blankly at the television screen.

"Jesus Christ," he whispered.

He fumbled his phone from his pocket and frantically dialed the monitoring room number.

The damn line was busy.

Hansen was out the door, down the stairs, and off toward CERN with a squeal of tires before the cat was out of the kitchen to see what all the excitement was about.

* * *

Sometimes timing is everything.

As Hansen came pounding in breathless through the doorway, the air at the center of the underground monitoring room softly popped.

Fritzie, just putting down the phone, looked from Hansen toward the sound. He slowly got to his feet.

Something very peculiar had just appeared at the center of the spreading sphere of ripples. It hung in the air, slowly turning, a shifting geometric form throwing rainbow lights. It was the soul of enticement itself.

Fritzie took a step forward, unconsciously raising his hand.

"Stop!" Hansen shouted. "Back away from it, Fritzie!"

The little German froze in his tracks. He broke his eyes free, slowly looking around toward Hansen, who was leaning against the door jamb, still trying to catch his breath.

"What?" said Fritzie. "What *is* it?"

Hansen's face had gone pale. He was staring at the object with an expression of mixed fascination and horror.

"We made ripples," Hansen said. "Somewhere something noticed."

Hansen's eyes shifted to Jeffries' coat and cup. He shut them tightly and shook his head, as if mere denial might hold some real power over reality. Then he looked back to Fritzie.

"I think it's some sort of a lure."

BIBLIOPHILES

From Rachel's Blog

Today was the sort of day that makes me thoughtful; a day when rain was falling, and the leaves on the trees trembled and dripped, and people hurried along the wet sidewalk with their collars turned up and their umbrellas in their hands. It's on days like that—when it's dim outside and we turn on the lights inside the bookstore—that I'll sometimes look toward the window and surprise my own reflection.

There's something about my reflection that always makes me thoughtful.

I have a friend. Her name is Felicia. Felicia tells me that her own reflection affects her much the same way. That's not at all surprising, I suppose, because Felicia and I have something very unusual in common. When we see ourselves in the window, it shows.

Felicia and I go way back; back to the day when we met at a certain college. The college was also where we met our good friend Pandora, and where we discovered that we all love books.

Pandora is what people call a *bibliophile*. She loves her books and she loves to read. She *especially* likes to read out loud. That's an important point. It was because of Pandora's habit of reading out loud that Felicia and I discovered that *we* were bibliophiles too.

That was a wonderful discovery! It was like opening a door on a whole new world! It's something that the three have in common, and the main reason that we all have the bookstore together.

Now, you mustn't think everything we discovered at the college was all that wonderful, or that everyone we met there was all that good, because that would be about as far from the truth as you could get. I suppose Felicia and I were really quite naïve, way back then. Before Pandora came along, the two of us had fallen in with the wrong sort of people. We certainly didn't know it at the time. We hadn't understood that bad things were beginning to happen, nor that something was *about* to happen that was so terrible I can hardly even bear to think about it now.

It was lucky for us that Pandora found out. Pandora didn't even think twice. She rescued us! We escaped! We all left the college and disappeared!

Pandora sometimes worries that the bad people might still be looking for us, even after all this time. The person that she worries the most about is Dr. Malpin.

Felicia says they've probably given up and forgotten all about us by now, but I'm afraid I agree with Pandora. Bad people can be *very* persistent.

Sometimes I have terrible dreams about Dr. Malpin.

I don't much like remembering any of that, much less telling someone about it. So, what else can I tell you?

OK, here's something:

I'm black. *Blacker than a black cat in a coal mine*, as they sometimes say, though I've never actually been inside of one.

Felicia, on the other hand, is white. Think of snow.

Felicia is also slender, and graceful, and has beautiful green eyes.

Really, Felicia's eyes are absolutely *beautiful*! Their color reminds me of the palest green jade. People comment about them all the time. Once in a while it makes me a little bit jealous, but that's just a girl thing.

Truth be told, Felicia and I love each other, and we're *both* in love with Pandora. Maybe I should explain how that came about.

I met Pandora first. Before Felicia did, I mean; Felicia and I already knew each other.

Pandora was studying English Literature at the college I told you about, and working nights at the Behavioral Research Center. Not much went on there after hours, so Pandora had a great deal of time to read, and I had a great deal of time to listen. English Literature, of course, wasn't the most practical thing for such a pretty girl to be studying, but Pandora didn't care. After we left the college Felicia and I realized this was a problem, so we put our heads together and solved it. Pandora thinks having the bookstore was *her* idea, but actually it was *ours*.

Anyway, it wasn't long before Pandora and I fell in love. Then Felicia, who'd been away to another part of the Center, came back. Felicia—being the total copycat that she is—promptly fell in love with Pandora too, and the next thing we knew Pandora was in love with the both of us.

So, there you go! We're all three beautiful, and we love each other, and we all share the apartment over the bookstore.

I'm wondering now what you might be thinking about that. If you've been paying close attention, there's probably no confusion at all; but if you haven't been, and if you're the narrow-minded sort, I suppose you *might* be thinking that you've discovered something worthy of your disapproval.

Well, if that's the case the joke is on you, and you can put it in your pipe and smoke it. But smoke it outside, please! We don't allow smoking in our bookstore.

Now we've come to something I've been waiting for:

Can you guess the name of our bookstore?

The answer is obvious, if you'll only think about it for a moment. Of course, obvious things are what people most often seem to miss.

Are you thinking?

It's on the sign outside, right over the big front window. A long, dark green sign, with BIG GOLD LETTERS . . .

Give up?

Pandora's Books!

We have a great many books at Pandora's Books. So many that Felicia and I have never really bothered to count them all, although I'm sure that Pandora knows.

Pandora is very good with organization and numbers and such, so that sort of thing is her main job. Pandora says Felicia and I are especially good at *dis*organization, and she may be right. An unfortunate tendency toward clutter and disorganization is a common trait amongst seriously afflicted bibliophiles.

Pandora keeps track of everything on our computer, which is on a table against the wall behind the counter.

That's where I'm sitting right now. I use the computer at night—which it happens to be at the moment—while Pandora is upstairs sleeping. I hide my special folders where Pandora won't find them. I really don't know *what* Pandora would think if she ever did.

Pandora spends much of each day sitting here, right where I'm sitting now, sorting through boxes of books, adding titles to our list and taking titles away, while Felicia and I tend to the walk-in customers.

Felicia and I are very good with customers, so tending to them is *our* main job. We're especially good at making subtle suggestions about which books they need and which books they really don't. Figuring that out and working our advice in without seeming to be meddlesome or presumptuous—most often without the customer ever even noticing what we're doing—is really something of an art. It's something all good booksellers know how to do.

Our computer has a high-speed cable connection. Other people at other computers can go through our list, find titles they want, and send us their orders. And Pandora can hunt through other bookstore lists to find the things that *we* want. Books are coming and going that way all the time. The brown UPS truck stops on the street outside our window twice a day, except on Saturdays and Sundays. On Saturdays the truck comes only once, and on Sundays not at all. On Sundays our bookstore is closed.

We all three like Sundays, because on that day we can stay in bed as long as we like. Some Sundays we stay there all morning. Pandora might read aloud from a book, while Felicia and I just lay back and listen. (Pandora not only loves to read out loud, but has a very good way with it.) Or maybe we'll watch old movies on the television. We each have our favorites, but there are some we all like. One of my

G. S. HARGRAVE

own favorites is *Bell, Book and Candle*, from 1958; we all like the 1933 version of *Little Women*. That's the one with Katharine Hepburn.

Pandora is also useful in the bookstore because she's so tall. She's almost as tall as Andy, who drives the UPS truck. Unlike Felicia or me, Pandora can reach the topmost book on the highest bookshelf with ease. Felicia and I have to climb up there.

About Andy: I'm pretty sure Andy has a thing for Pandora, but Pandora seems not to have noticed.

Something else about that: Andy doesn't seem to have noticed that there's anything different about Pandora and Felicia and me.

It's not that Pandora makes a secret of things. She just doesn't wear a sign on her sleeve. I would think most anyone who met us would realize, but the truth is they usually don't.

Remember what I said about people missing the obvious?

I think Felicia is a bit jealous about Andy liking Pandora, and a little bit suspicious of him, too. Felicia seems aloof whenever Andy comes in, always drifting away to take care of something or other toward the back of the bookstore, but I've caught her watching him closely when she thought no one was looking.

I'm not one to get jealous, myself. Only a little over the way people go on about how beautiful Felicia's eyes are, maybe, or about Pandora's dexterous fingers. In my heart of hearts, I know where Felicia and I stand with Pandora, every bit as much as I know where Felicia and I stand with each other.

You might be wondering what sort of books we sell in our bookstore. I certainly hope so, because I'm going to tell you! Of course, if you have a computer you could simply pull up our store list, but that wouldn't be nearly so much fun. Besides, there are a number of bookstores called Pandora's Books. I know exactly how many, because I looked it up on the internet.

Ours is a bookstore for bibliophiles, and they're different from people who simply like to read. They're an entirely different breed of cat, you might say. For bibliophiles, it's not just about what's in the book, it's about the book itself.

What I'm referring to here are things like the tightness and fineness of bindings, the color of cloth or leather, the quality of the paper inside and the way the print looks on the page. All of those things can be beautifully or poorly done. If any of them were poorly done with some particular edition of some particular book, you probably won't find that edition in our bookstore—unless, of course, there's something else very special about it.

Another thing: All of our books were previously owned. This is an important point, because well-made books become even better when they've been owned by someone who loved them.

That's something about a book that I can always tell. Felicia says it's one of my *special talents*, and she may be right. I seem to pick up on all sorts of things that Pandora and Felicia miss. They're both very intuitive, but *I* have *intuition plus.*

Sometimes we find things that previous owners have left inside their books. You'd be surprised what we find! Sometimes there might be something that makes me happy, but other times there might be something that makes me sad. For example:

Once we found an old love letter. It was in an edition of

Shelly's Poems, published by Thomas Y. Crowell & Co., No. 13 Astor Place, New York, 1878. (I have a very good memory for details, don't I?) I liked the book, with its ornately embossed binding and engraved illustrations and gilt edges. The pages had red borders, and a red silk ribbon was sewn in to serve as a bookmark. The writing on the letter was faded, written by a young woman who'd had a lovely, old-fashion hand.

Pandora read the letter aloud. It was a happy letter, full of hopes and promises—but there it was, tucked away forever inside a dusty old book that the woman herself had owned. (We knew that because she'd written her name on the flyleaf in the same beautiful hand.) So, the letter had never been sent. It held a dim echo of missed chances and regrets that made me feel sad.

It must have made Pandora feel sad too, because she was very quiet for the rest of the afternoon. Felicia and I left Pandora alone for a while and took care of the bookstore ourselves.

Another time we found a violet, folded up inside a bit of yellowed Japan paper. It had been pressed inside *The Goblin Market*, by Christina Georgina Rossetti, published by McMillan & Co. of London, 1893—a slim edition, with intricate Art Nouveau ornamentation. (Felicia says I like to show off just how good my memory is, but it's really only that I love the small details.) The violet was faded, but there was still a tiny trace of color left in it. For just an instant I had a clear picture in my mind of a long-ago afternoon, and of the girl who had put the violet there. She had been very happy that afternoon, and a little of her happiness was left in the flower, so it made me happy when we found it.

Pandora has a policy about the things we find in old books: We must leave them where we find them. They're part of the history of the book now, she says, making their journeys through time, traveling in their books as if in little ships. Our bookstore is only a place where they've paused, not their destination.

This makes perfect sense to Felicia and me, so we're all in complete agreement.

The books in our store are shelved by category. (I do like that word.) We have everything from *Apiculture* to *Zymurgy*, with a great many things in between. (Pandora likes certain words too, but I think those are a bit too cryptic for the labels on bookstore shelves; *Beekeeping* and *Winemaking* would probably be better, in my opinion.) Within each labeled category our books are alphabetized by author.

Except, of course, for the *Really Special* books. Books on the *Really Special* shelves are arranged in no particular order. That's deliberate. The *Really Special* shelves are where the most seriously afflicted bibliophiles tend to look first, and they seem to like the randomness. Maybe it heightens their sense that they're *on the hunt*—which, I suppose, is something that I can very naturally appreciate.

What makes a book *Really Special* is no one particular thing. It might be especially old, or especially beautiful, or it may be neither of those things but have some entirely unique history about it.

We once had a late 1920's edition of *Beowulf*, for example. The text was Anglo-Saxon. While the book itself was not especially old, and certainly not especially beautiful, a certain British philologist had jotted down notes in all the margins. His curious handwriting was immediately recognizable. That one thing alone qualified the book for a place of honor on the *Really Special* shelves.

We have a lot of books shelved under *The Sciences.*

Most are obscure editions, and many are quite difficult. We also have a large selection of books in the *Metaphysical and Occult* category. Those books fill up an entire section. Trust me on this: They aren't the sort of books you might find in your local big name bookstore.

That's just another detail in a world made out of details, but some details are a lot more significant than others. Have you taken note of that one?

People do so often miss the obvious.

OK, enough for now.

Something in the Rain

I first saw the shadow on the sort of day that I told you about before. I told you just after you figured out that there was someone named Rachel, and that the someone named Rachel was me. Do you remember what I said?

Well, this was another day when it was raining, and we had the lights turned on inside the bookstore. It was just the sort of day when I might have surprised my reflection, but I didn't. Instead, something surprised *me*.

There was no one else in the bookstore on this particular day. Andy had brought us our books before the rain had started, and Pandora and Felicia were sitting on the Oriental rug between the leather reading chairs, going through the new boxes. I was sitting on the edge of the counter near the register as I sometimes do, watching the rain through the bookstore's big front window.

A black car went by on the street outside, its windshield wipers working hard against the slanting drops. The car splashed water up from a puddle as it passed, and then the car was gone.

That was when I saw it. I saw its shape in the air by

where the splashed up water hadn't gone.

I watched it for a moment, outlined now by the falling rain drops, wondering what it might be. Clearly it was something very odd. It was certainly more than something not really there at all.

I glanced around toward Pandora and Felicia to see if maybe they had seen, but they hadn't. They were still on the floor with the new boxes of books. They were looking at one book in particular—an oddly heavy book, Pandora had said, that she couldn't remember having ordered. Pandora was reading something out loud that had been penned on the final few pages, which had been left empty of any printed text. The ink was yellowish-brown and the inscription lengthy; the words sounded strange and had a very peculiar sort of rhythm to them.

I suppose I might have gotten their attention then, but I didn't. I had never seen something only a little bit more than not really there at all before, and I didn't want to seem foolish.

I slid down from my place on the counter and walked casually over to the big front window. I casually hopped up onto the low window ledge, where we display a few books for people to see as they walk by on the sidewalk, and casually looked back outside.

The empty place in the rain was still there, but it had moved while I wasn't looking. Before, it had been at the outer edge of the sidewalk, alongside the dark green parking meter. Now it had crept across the sidewalk and was much closer to the glass.

I didn't like that I hadn't seen the shadow-thing move. I *especially* didn't like that it had moved closer. Moving closer without being noticed is one of my own games, but with the shape in the rain there was something about it that didn't feel at all like playing.

Felicia must have noticed that I was watching something then, because she came over and hopped up beside me. I glanced at her. When I looked back out through the window again the shape in the rain had gone.

Later, after Pandora had locked the front door and gone upstairs and put on a CD and started to make dinner, I told Felicia about the shadow. I told her how I hadn't liked it.

"What did it look like, Rachel?"

"It didn't look like anything at all," I said.

Felicia's green eyes narrowed. "It couldn't have looked like nothing at all if you *saw* it."

"I saw the place where it was; an outline in the rain; a place where the raindrops didn't go."

"Maybe, then, it was something you only imagined. Like the mouse in the storeroom . . ." Felicia put on her most serious look.

"The shape in the rain was *real*," I said. After a moment I added: "So was the mouse."

Felicia was teasing me. She had conceded a long while back that there might really have been a mouse. Felicia said there was a secret way in and out of the bookstore, from a dark place in the basement where they had once kept coal. She said she'd squeezed through there once and looked out into the alley. That might be where the mouse got in.

"Do you think you might have seen it without the rain?" Felicia had seen I wasn't playing. Now she was *really* being serious.

"I don't think so," I said. "I wouldn't have known to look."

Felicia thought that over. "What about now that you *do* know?"

"Now that we know it's there, I think we might see it

even without the rain. I'm not sure, but I think we might."

"Then we must *watch* for it," Felicia said. "It might be something bad. We mustn't let anything bad come into the bookstore!"

* * *

Pandora was looking at us thoughtfully. "You two have been quiet lately."

It had taken Pandora a couple of days to notice something was different. The difference was that Felicia and I were being watchful. I was sitting on the front counter next to the cash register, keeping an eye on the door; Felicia was sitting on the ledge keeping watch out the front window. She didn't even bother to turn around.

Pandora gave me a questioning look. Then she shrugged and turned back to the computer and read what she'd typed so far. Soon she was clicking away at the keyboard again.

Pandora can type very quickly—much faster than I can. I enjoy listening to the sound her fingers make as they dance across the keys. Sometimes I close my eyes to listen even better, but at the moment I was watching the words that were appearing on the screen.

Pandora was writing to another bookseller, who keeps another bookshop far away in a place called Newport, Rhode Island. She was trying to find out about the book she couldn't remember having ordered. The book had become something of a puzzle. The title wasn't on the internet. Neither was the name of the author, or the name of the company that had published it.

Pandora finished her e-mail. She read it over, tapped the button to send it off, and got up to get herself another cup of tea.

Pandora certainly likes her tea. She carries her cup

around with her all day. I don't care for tea in the least.

"She's noticed," Felicia said.

"Of course she's noticed," I said. "She just doesn't know *what* she's noticed."

You might think we would have simply told Pandora about what I'd seen outside the window, but things really don't work that way. Telling something to Pandora isn't as simple as you might think.

During the time since the black car had gone by, neither Felicia nor I had seen anything the least bit unusual. I think maybe Felicia was becoming skeptical again about the thing that almost wasn't there at all, but if she was she hadn't said anything about it.

Later that afternoon a reply came to Pandora's message. I was sitting on the counter again and I read it over Pandora's shoulder. The Newport bookseller didn't know a thing about the book Pandora couldn't remember having ordered. She said it had never been on her inventory list, and she had no idea how it had come to be in the box. She didn't know anything about the author or publisher, either.

Later still, Pandora came back and read the e-mail again. There wasn't any more to read than there had been the first time, but she read it again anyway, because that was where things had stopped making sense to her. I guess it was kind of like the way I kept going back to the place where I thought I had seen the mouse.

Pandora brought up the screen she uses to add things to our inventory list. She typed in the details of the book: *Thoughtforms in Theory and Practice*; Garmund Firth, Ph.D.; Oculus Publications, London, 1873. She stopped when she got to the place where she had to enter a price.

Pandora read over what she'd typed, and then she

turned and looked at me. I saw the little between-the-eyebrows crease Pandora gets when she's thinking or puzzled or worrying about something. She pursed her lips and turned back to the computer. Then she deleted what she had typed without entering it.

After we'd closed for the day, Pandora took the book upstairs and put it on the nightstand. Later, after she got into bed, she picked up the book and turned on the lamp.

I had seen right away that the book might be *really special*. For one thing, it was the author's own copy; his personalized bookplate was inside, having a peculiar looking design with an eye at the center and rays coming out of it, as if it were a picture of the sun. The book was full of hand-written commentary he'd added in the margins. There was also the long inscription on the final unprinted pages, and the complicated diagram he'd drawn inside the back cover. The diagram had lots of odd symbols—like the strange things you might see in a book about quantum physics—with strange words circling around it in an odd-looking script. The diagram was in black ink, but the strange symbols and words had faded to yellowish-brown, just like the long, handwritten inscription. We have old handwritten journals and monographs in the store where the ink has faded like that.

For some reason the diagram made me feel creepy.

Pandora read from the book for a while, reading the interesting parts out loud as she usually does. Felicia fell asleep, but I stayed awake to listen.

Garmund Firth had been a Professor of Oriental Studies. In the introduction, he claimed to have spent many years traveling and studying all sorts of mysterious things in far-away places like India and Tibet. This particular book was mostly about *tulpas*.

A tulpa, according to Firth, is a sort of *thoughtform*: a living being created by the power of the mind, or the power of a person's will, or whatever. It's something imagined so very strongly that it's imagined right into reality.

Sometimes, Firth said, a tulpa might be made by accident; other times it's done on purpose. It might be poorly imagined and wispy and ghostlike, quickly fading away; or it might be so solid that it can't be told from something that's really real. Tulpas can take the shape of people or animals or almost anything.

Sometimes a person who makes a tulpa loses control of it, and it goes off on its own and creates all sorts of trouble. Garmund Firth told a story about a Tibetan monk who created a tulpa that looked just like the monk himself, but then he couldn't get rid of it. According to the story, the tulpa followed the poor monk around from place to place, and finally *murdered* him.

That, I suppose, is what they call *a cautionary tale*.

Firth provided a long series of *Lessons and Exercises*, gradually working up to the actual creation of a tulpa. At the end—before the blank pages to which he'd added the long, handwritten part—Firth explained about *Banishment*, which is how you get rid of what you've created.

Having heard the cautionary tale, I would have thought that last part should have come first.

Pandora turned to the handwritten part that had been added to the final unprinted pages and read some of it. I was struck again by how very odd it sounded. Partway through, she yawned. She closed the book and put it on the nightstand. Then, after arranging her pillows *just so* as she always does, she reached over and clicked off the lamp.

Before long Pandora was sound asleep and Felicia was waking up. We jumped down off of the bed and went downstairs to the bookstore.

Pandora thinks we sleep on the bed all night. She thinks so because we're almost always asleep beside her when she wakes up in the morning.

There's *a lot* Pandora doesn't know.

The bookstore is a very different place at night. It's dim and shadowy and mysterious. There are little glowing lights where the computer is, and there's the light that comes in through the big front window from the lamppost across the street. Sometimes there's moonlight, too, which is an altogether different sort of light. The tree on our side of the street throws shadows through the window. When there's a breeze the shadows move around and make the inside of the bookstore seem alive.

Felicia went over to look out the front window. She likes to look at the moon and to see what might be going on out there. One time we saw a coyote, big as you please, right there on the deserted city street. It was trotting along, glancing quickly from side to side. It looked hungry and fast and terribly dangerous.

I went over to the desk behind the counter and nudged the mouse thing with my nose to wake up the computer. I thought I would write something for my blog. For a while I just sat there, thinking about what I might write.

"Rachel!" Felicia's voice wasn't loud, but something about the way she said my name *seemed* loud. She turned back to the window the instant I looked up.

I got down off the computer chair and jumped up beside Felicia on the window ledge.

"Across the street," she whispered. "By the streetlamp."

At first I didn't see anything, but then I did. It was like the shadow of a man, but without the man to go with it.

"Is that what you saw before?" she asked.

"That's it!" I said. "But now it looks more solid!"

As we watched, I suddenly realized that the shadow was watching us back. It was a feeling I had, but one that was very certain and specific, like what I sometimes get when we find something inside of an old book.

The shadow rippled and slipped away from the lamppost. It slid across the street toward us—not at all like something walking, but like something gliding over a sheet of ice. It paused beside the parking meter; then it slid across the sidewalk until it was right outside the window. The glass turned cold. I could see my breath on it.

I could feel Felicia's tension. She was as tense as a clock spring wound up so tight that it was about ready to snap. "What *is* it?" she whispered.

"Did you hear what Pandora read earlier?"

"Some of it," she said. "Part of the time I might have been dreaming."

"I think it's a *tulpa*," I said. "I think it's getting more real. That probably means somebody made it on purpose, and *sent* it here."

"Who would *do* something like that?" Felicia spoke so quietly that I could scarcely hear her. I think she was afraid that the thing outside the window might be able to hear her, too.

I glanced at her. "Dr. Malpin? What if Dr. Malpin found us? Maybe *he* sent that thing."

Felicia shivered with her entire body. "Do you think it could . . . *hurt* us?"

"I don't think it's real enough," I said. "Not yet."

"We've got to tell Pandora, Rachel! We've got to warn her!"

"How? How can we tell Pandora? How could we explain to her?"

112

"*You* know how," Felicia said.

Felicia was right: I *did* know how. It was just that the idea of it frightened me almost as much as the thing outside the window. Now everything would have to change.

The Broken Teacup

How to do it was actually the simple part: I made another entry to my blog, but this time I didn't hide anything. I left the page open on the computer screen. It would be the first thing Pandora would see in the morning when she sat down at the computer and moved the mouse and the screen saver went away.

The next morning started the same as usual. Pandora woke up and found us on the bed where we always are. She got up and had her shower and got dressed and made our breakfasts, and then we all had them, and then Pandora made her first cup of tea and we all went downstairs to open the bookstore. Pandora unlocked the door and raised the door blind and turned the sign around so CLOSED showed on the inside and OPEN showed on the outside. Then she sat down at our computer and moved the mouse.

For a while nothing happened. Pandora just sat there reading. I heard a mouse click. She leaned closer to the monitor and read some more. Then she jerked back in her chair and the teacup hit the floor and broke and tea spread across the polished floorboards all the way over to the Oriental carpet.

For a long time Pandora didn't move. When she finally reached for the mouse, her hand was shaking. Every now and then I heard another click. She was going from one page of my blog to another.

She didn't say anything for a very long time. At last she

slowly turned around and looked at me, where I was waiting on the counter.

"*Rachel?*" Pandora's voice was just a tiny little squeak.

Felicia hopped up on the counter and sat down beside me, and we both sat there together, watching Pandora.

"*Now* she knows," Felicia said.

Pandora looked quickly at Felicia, almost as if she'd heard something.

"She probably thinks she's going crazy," I said. "Poor Pandora!"

Pandora quickly looked at me, the little crease showing between her eyebrows. This, I thought, might be the time when the little crease finally stuck. She put her hands up to either side of her face, slowly shaking her head. "I must be going crazy," she said.

I slowly turned my head from side to side, keeping my eyes on Pandora's. I knew this was an entirely un-catlike thing to do—that it would probably be very disturbing—but I had to make sure that Pandora understood.

Pandora looked down at the broken teacup and the tea that had splashed out across the floor. The edge of the carpet was getting wet. She frowned. She picked up the pieces of her favorite china teacup and dropped them into the wastebasket, and then she went to the storeroom and got a towel and came back and wiped up the spilt tea.

The front door opened and Andy the UPS man came in. He smiled and said "Hello" to Pandora, and then he said "Hello" to Felicia and me, and then put down some boxes where he usually puts them down. Then he stopped. Pandora was watching him with the towel in her hand, and Felicia and I were watching him from the counter. He looked back and forth between us.

"Uh . . . Everything's OK?"

Pandora put her hand up to her head. She scrunched her eyes shut for a moment. She didn't seem able to formulate a reply. What was she supposed to say?

"Everything's *fine*." Pandora looked at the floor. "I broke a teacup. It got the carpet wet. I . . ." She stopped and looked at Felicia and me. "I don't think it will stain." Then she looked at Andy and just stood there, as if she had no clue what to do next. I suppose that was pretty much the situation. We were all watching Andy as if he were a visitor from Mars.

"OK," Andy said, drawing both syllables waaay out. He didn't look so certain. "I'll see you tomorrow, then." Halfway out he paused and glanced back, then the door closed and he got into his UPS truck and drove away.

Pandora went over to the front door. She locked it and turned the sign around and pulled down the blind. She gave Felicia and me a long, strange, scary look, and then she went upstairs, still carrying the stupid towel.

We decided it might be best to leave Pandora alone for a while, until she'd had time to think things through and decide that she wasn't going crazy. Pandora is a logical girl, so we knew she'd figure it out sooner or later.

It also seemed best to leave Pandora alone because she'd shut the stairway door behind her on her way upstairs. I'd heard the lock click.

* * *

It was almost dark when we finally heard the lock at the bottom of the stairs turn again, and saw the door open partway. Pandora went back up the stairs without saying a word. Felicia and I looked at each other, and then we went up the stairs after her.

Pandora gave us our dinner. We all had poached fish, which was very good, and Pandora had some bread and

115

some wine with hers. She still hadn't said anything. She just kept watching us, which was beginning to make us both feel nervous.

After dinner, Pandora cleared away the dishes and went into the bedroom. We could hear her from the kitchen, rummaging around in the bedroom closet. When she came back she was carrying a flat box. She put it on the table and took off the lid and took something out. It looked like a game. Felicia and I jumped up on the chairs to watch.

"What's that?" Felicia asked.

"I think I know," I said. "It's a ouija board!"

Felicia hopped up on the table for a closer look. Usually we got scolded when we got up on the table, but things were different this evening. Felicia sat down. "What does it do?"

"People put their hands on that pointy thing and ask it questions," I said. "Then they slide it around and it spells out the answers."

"That's dumb."

Felicia obviously didn't get it, but after she looked at the board and saw the words and letters she realized what Pandora was up to. Felicia was at one corner of the board, so I hopped up on the table and sat down at the other. We both looked across at Pandora and Pandora looked back at us. She filled her glass again. Pandora was having more wine than she usually does. She sat up very straight on the ladder-back chair and composed herself.

"OK," she said. She closed her eyes and shook her head. "I've completely popped my cork, haven't I?"

She'd said that to herself, of course, but it was a question. I put my foot on the slider and pushed it until it pointed to the word *No*.

Pandora didn't move. She started to say something, but stopped. She was staring at the pointer thing. "You . . . You both understand every word I'm saying?"

I put out my foot again and moved the pointer to *Yes*.

"And you use the computer at night, and that's Rachel's blog on the internet, and you think I'm a witch and you're my familiars." Pandora was getting a strange look in her eyes again.

I left the slider where it was and tapped it once.

"*Jesus on a bicycle,*" Pandora whispered.

"What does she mean by that?" Felicia asked, and Pandora looked at Felicia.

"I have no idea," I replied, and Pandora looked at me.

That's when we all suddenly realized Pandora could actually hear us now. I'm not sure how it happened. Maybe Pandora had been able to all along, but had just that moment gotten to the point where she realized it. Maybe up until then it had seemed so crazy that she couldn't allow herself to think about it.

Or maybe it was like seeing the shadow. First you had to know it was there, and then you had to know how to look.

* * *

It was very early in the morning and I was very upset. Felicia had gone into the bedroom and fallen asleep, but Pandora and I had stayed up to talk things over. Pandora had been telling me that things weren't at all the way I thought.

"I'm really not a witch, baby. You and Felicia aren't my familiars. It isn't like the *Bell, Book and Candle* movie. That was just a movie, not something real."

"So what *is* it like then, Pandora?"

"I don't know," she said. "It's not like anything I've ever thought about before."

"And Dr. Malpin isn't an evil warlock . . ."

117

"No, Rachel. Dr. Malpin is a *scientist*. I don't think he's evil. Just . . . dangerous."

"He wanted to *kill Felicia*," I said. "He wanted to look at her brain!"

"Yes, that's true. Sometimes people don't understand how bad something is. Sometimes they get so focused on one thing that they lose track of everything else. I think maybe it was like that with Dr. Malpin. That's why I took you away."

"What about the shadow outside the window?" I said. "Felicia and I *both* saw it."

"I'm . . . not sure about all of the things they did at the Behavioral Research Center. I only worked there for a few months. I was only an *attendant*, Rachel. I know you and Felicia were part of an experiment. I know that you're both transgenic." She looked at me for a moment. "Do you know what that word means?"

I nodded. I had looked the word up on the computer.

"So, you're both different than anything that's ever been before. It's possible . . ." Pandora glanced down, and then back up. "In some ways, Rachel, you're like children. To be honest, I'm not sure how rational you are. It's possible that you might imagine things. Like the movie made you imagine that I'm a witch, or like the book made you imagine there was a tulpa."

"I saw the shadow *before* I figured out what the book was about," I said. "I can imagine *all sorts of things*, Pandora, but I know what's real! I'm not entirely sure that *you* do."

Pandora raised her eyebrows and sat back in her chair. Her cat was talking back.

"Felicia and I aren't just one of Dr. Malpin's *accidents*," I said. "And *you're* not just some girl who works in a

118

bookstore. How do you think you can hear us? Is that the usual thing, Pandora? For girls who work in bookstores to hear their cats talking?"

The little crease in Pandora's forehead was back. "It's *you*, not *me*," she said. "You're neurologically different. You're . . . telepathic or something."

Well, *sure*, I thought. *That* certainly explains it. We were most definitely *or something.*

"And I'm *angry* with you, Rachel," Pandora went on. Her color had come up a bit. Maybe she'd had too much wine. "You should have asked before you used our computer. And a blog! That was dangerous! What if Dr. Malpin or somebody at the Behavioral Research Center saw it? It might help them find us!"

"How would I have asked?" I said. "Besides, Dr. Malpin never knew our names. I was just Specimen TGF-48 and Felicia was just Specimen TGF-52. That's what it said on our cages. We were just *specimens*, Pandora! *You* gave us our names, remember?" Then I said: "What's Dr. Malpin going to do, Pandora? Google for talking cats? He never knew we could do that. You didn't even know yourself!"

I had blurted out all of that to hold up my end of the argument, but I suppose I was trying to reassure myself, too. Actually, I hadn't thought about Dr. Malpin seeing the blog before, and what Pandora had just said had frightened me.

Pandora folded her arms and gave me her hard look, but then her eyes softened and she sighed. "Look, Rachel, it's just . . . This is kind of hard for me to take in all at once, you know?"

"I know, Pandora. Maybe you should get some sleep. Maybe it will make more sense in the morning."

Pandora nodded, so we went to bed. Pandora fell asleep

very quickly and snored softly after she did. She doesn't usually snore. I think maybe it was because of all the wine she'd had. She'd had four glasses!

I secretly sampled some of Pandora's wine once, when she'd gone out of the living room for a moment. I didn't like the way it tasted at all.

As soon as Pandora was asleep, Felicia woke up. She yawned and had a big stretch, and then we both went downstairs and sat on the window ledge. We looked up and down the street. There was nothing out of the ordinary. I told Felicia about the long talk I'd had with Pandora.

"I didn't think she would believe there was a shadow," Felicia said. "The shadow is just one new thing too many." She glanced back toward the window, about to say something else, but suddenly she froze. I looked where Felicia was looking.

It was there again.

Now it was even more distinct, even more solid. As we watched, it slid across the street toward where we sat behind the glass. I could see it was beginning to have a face.

Felicia's eyes got very wide. We both jumped off the ledge and quickly retreated away from the window, to watch from the darkness between the bookcases.

The shadow crossed the sidewalk. It reached out one hand and then the other, feeling around the glass high and low, pressing close to the pane, exploring the window and the frame all around it. We could see that it was trying to figure out how to get in.

It couldn't. It moved away from the window and paused, and then it drifted back across the street. Felicia and I jumped back up on the ledge to watch. It took steps like a person now, but it still slid smoothly along the pavement in a different way than real steps would account for. It reached the lamp post and then it disappeared into the darkness.

* * *

Pandora woke up grumpy. I blame the wine. After a stop in the bathroom she headed for the kitchen. She glanced at the ouija board and shook her head and put on the kettle.

Felicia woke up while Pandora was showering. Pandora got dressed and made breakfast for us just like always. She still hadn't said anything, but she was clearly in a better mood after her first cup of tea. By the time we all went downstairs to open the bookstore, I could see that things between us were probably going to be OK.

It certainly wasn't a busy morning, probably because of more rainy November weather. We had the lights on and Pandora had turned up the heat. Now she was at the computer. She checked her e-mails and tended to some routine business while I sat on the counter and watched. After that, she brought up my blog again. I hadn't realized she had bookmarked it.

"This is really very good, Rachel," she said after a while. She turned around in her chair and looked at me. "I'm proud of you! Maybe you should think about becoming a writer."

I was so flustered that I didn't know what to say. Being a writer was one of my secret ambitions, and I was surprised at how good what Pandora said made me feel.

"Now she'll be even more stuck on herself than she was before," Felicia commented from the window ledge.

That was what they call *a catty remark*, but I knew it was all in fun. Felicia had read my blog before and had told me she liked my writing.

Pandora got up to make some more tea. We have a machine downstairs that heats water for her tea and makes coffee for our customers, but there wasn't any tea left in the box she keeps under the counter. I watched her go up the stairs to get some from the kitchen cupboard. I could hear her walking around up there.

The front door opened and shut behind me. I glanced around to see who had come in, but whoever it was had stepped behind the end of the bookshelf just inside, where we have a pin board for our Local Events Calendar and announcements and such. All I could see was the edge of a long dark coat. Felicia had looked around too, from her place on the window ledge.

I watched the edge of the dark coat for a moment. Suddenly I began to get a very strange feeling. I glanced over toward Felicia. She was backing away along the window ledge, looking toward the end of the bookshelf where I couldn't see. Her ears were down flat and her tail was bushed out and the fur along her back was beginning to stand up.

Just then I heard Pandora coming down the stairs and at the same moment the front door opened again and Andy came in with a box of books. The edge of the dark coat vanished. I caught a glimpse of the black coat through the front window, hurrying along the sidewalk, flapping in the wind and rain like a bat. Lightning flickered and thunder rumbled as it passed, just like in a scary movie.

Felicia shot past below me toward the storeroom. I jumped down from the counter and followed her.

Felicia was huddled in a dark corner behind some boxes. I could hear Andy and Pandora talking out in the bookstore. Andy said something and Pandora laughed, and then Pandora said something back. It was as though nothing at all had happened.

"It was the shadow!" said Felicia. She was still

trembling. "Rachel, *it came inside!*"

I remembered the strange feeling I'd had, so I didn't doubt her for a moment. "What did it look like?" I asked. "Was it completely solid? Did it look like Dr. Malpin?"

"At first it was as solid as anything," Felicia said. "It was a tall, thin, pale man, with black hair and dark eyes, dressed all in black. Then it got a little bit see-through." Felicia glanced nervously toward the open storeroom door, and then she looked back at me. "It didn't look at all like Dr. Malpin." She shuddered. "Its eyes were *empty*, Rachel. It looked right at me, *and its eyes were cold and empty!*"

I imagined that in my mind and I shuddered too. "I saw the edge of its coat," I said. "Then I saw it go past the window outside after Andy came in."

"It can *get in* now, Rachel! What does it *want? What are we going to do?*"

"We're going to figure that out," I said. "I don't know how, but we're going to figure it all out. This is *our* place, and *nothing* is going to take it away from us!"

Through the Mouse Hole

Later that evening, we told Pandora about the Shadow Man coming into the bookstore. Pandora was sure that what we'd seen had only been someone who had come in to get out of the rain and then had gone away. We couldn't convince her.

I remembered what Pandora had said to me before, about not being sure how our minds worked. She hadn't said anything like that this time, but I knew she was thinking it. Before, she had said that we were like children. Now she was probably thinking that both of her cats were a little bit crazy.

After Pandora had gone to bed and fallen asleep, Felicia and I went downstairs. Felicia jumped up on the window ledge to keep watch, while I woke up the computer. I looked on the internet for anything that I could find out about Dr. Malpin and the Behavioral Research Center.

I found the Center's website, with a photograph of Dr. Malpin. He was still head of the program and looked much as I remembered him, except now he looked older.

I read everything, looking up all of the hard scientific words that I didn't understand. Dr. Malpin said he hoped his research would someday help people with neurological disorders. He had been doing things with genes, it said, trying to increase the number of neurons in the brain and the number of dendrites, which are the things that connect the neurons together.

Felicia and I weren't just transgenic, as it turned out. Dr. Malpin had been using his computers to make up and put together *entirely new* genetic sequences. Since there didn't seem to be a proper word for what you get when you do that, I made up a new one of my own: Felicia and I are *synthegenic.*

Now I wasn't so sure about Dr. Malpin. He didn't seem like the sort of person who would know about magic or tulpas. He seemed more like someone who wouldn't believe in anything like that at all. Scientists are wonderfully clever, you know, but they do seem to have trouble with things they haven't yet figured out how to be scientific about.

Was Dr. Malpin evil? I could see that he was trying to do something good, but I also knew he was doing some very bad things along the way. Scientists are responsible for the things under their care, aren't they? If they've made something new, they're *even more* responsible. And if that something is alive, and can think and feel, it certainly isn't

124

theirs to do with as they wish. Anyone should know that.

I told Felicia what I'd read.

"So what now, Rachel? If Dr. Malpin didn't send the Shadow Man, where could it have come from?"

"I don't know," I said. "If we knew where it went when it left here, maybe we could figure that out." I was thinking really hard, but it didn't seem to be helping.

"It's out there now," Felicia said.

I jumped down from Pandora's chair and went over to the window. The Shadow Man was across the street again—now looking much more like a man than a shadow. Its long black coat was blowing in the wind. That was all that moved.

"It's watching us," Felicia whispered. I could tell she was afraid. So was I.

"I think that's all it's going to do," I said, trying to sound reassuring. "If it's completely solid now, it can't get in with the door locked tight. Nothing can happen until morning."

"We can't just wait, Rachel. Something *really bad* is going to happen. I can feel it! We've got to do something!"

"What?" I said. "What can we do?"

Felicia looked back out across the street. "I can go outside through the secret way. I can follow it. I can see where it goes."

"*NO!*" I said, terribly alarmed. "You mustn't even *say* that! I don't like it! And Pandora wouldn't like it at all!"

"Pandora won't know," Felicia replied. "And don't you dare tell her!" She jumped down from the window ledge and started for the storeroom, where the stairs leading down to the basement are.

I was panicking and didn't know what to do. I thought about running upstairs and waking up Pandora, but I knew Felicia would be gone by then, so I followed Felicia into the

125

storeroom and down the stairs and through the creepy basement with the creepy old furnace and into the dark place where they used to keep the coal, arguing with her all the way, but it didn't do the least bit of good. There's simply no talking Felicia out of something, once she's made her mind up.

Felicia jumped up on some crates and from there up onto a concrete ledge. Then she squeezed into a narrow tunnel where some old iron pipes went back through the wall.

I tried to follow her, but I wouldn't fit.

If cats could cry I would have, but they can't, so I didn't.

I ran back upstairs to the bookstore as quickly as I could and jumped up on the window ledge. The Shadow Man thing was still across the street, exactly where it had been before. I watched it, almost forgetting to breathe. Then I saw Felicia. She was on the other side of the street now, hidden from the Shadow Man's view underneath the big blue mailbox. She must have gone down the alley and come out around the corner, crossing to the other side where the Shadow Man wouldn't see.

After a long time the Shadow Man turned and started off down the street. It walked like a man now, rather than sliding along. Someone might see it now and never even suspect that it *wasn't* a man.

Felicia waited, and then she came out from under the mailbox and followed after it. She was so good at keeping hidden that I almost didn't see her myself. I soon lost sight of her.

* * *

I hadn't slept all night. First I'd watched at the window for Felicia to come back, but she hadn't. Then I'd tried again to get out through the secret way, but of course I still couldn't, so I went back to the window and watched some more. I decided to wake up Pandora, and then I decided I shouldn't, because I thought surely Felicia would be back before morning. At last I went upstairs and lay down on the bed close to Pandora.

When Pandora woke up she noticed Felicia wasn't there, but that didn't seem too odd to her, so she had her shower and got dressed and made breakfast. When Felicia didn't come for her breakfast, though, Pandora frowned, and then she noticed that I wasn't eating mine. That's when she asked me where Felicia was, and that's when I told Pandora everything.

Pandora got really frightened. She was so frightened she didn't even think to get angry with me for not telling her before. Pandora could see that I was frightened too.

She hurried downstairs to go out and look for Felicia. I wanted to go with her, but Pandora told me it would be better if I waited at the bookstore in case Felicia came back. She locked the front door behind her and rushed off down the sidewalk.

After she left, I realized that this was the first time I could remember ever being alone. The bookstore seemed terribly empty and terribly quiet, and I began to think about how it would be if Felicia never came back. Once I started thinking about that I couldn't stop.

Hours crept by. Sometimes people tried the door to the bookstore and found it locked. Sometimes they put their hands up against the sides of their faces to peer in through the window before going away. A couple of times the telephone rang and rang, and then stopped ringing. Pandora had forgotten to turn on the answering machine. None of that interested me. None of it mattered. I just sat in the

127

front window and looked out, or went down to the basement and looked at the place where Felicia had gone out, or went upstairs and looked at the empty apartment. Everything I did only made me feel worse.

Finally, late in the morning, I heard the key in the lock and ran to the door. Pandora came in. She just shook her head and went upstairs without saying anything. When she came back down she sat on her computer chair and looked at me. We both just sat there for a while, and then the front door opened.

"Lose somebody?" It was Andy, and he had Felicia! "I tried to call you on my cell, but nobody answered."

Pandora ran over and took her.

If cats could cry, I would have been crying too.

* * *

"I was so busy following the Shadow Man I forgot to keep track of where I was going," Felicia said. She'd just had her breakfast. It was very late for breakfast, and Felicia hadn't stopped eating until she'd finished every bit of it. I'd just had mine too. We'd both been very hungry.

"I wandered all around," she said, "but nothing looked at all familiar. I didn't know the names of any of the streets. I walked for blocks and blocks. Then I saw Andy's truck by the sidewalk, so I waited until he came back. He recognized me right away and brought me home." Felicia looked at Pandora. "Andy was worried about how worried *you* must be, Pandora. I think he likes you."

Pandora frowned. "This has *got* to stop!" she said. She was very cross. "I want you both to promise me you'll *never* go outside like that again."

"I won't," Felicia promised. "I didn't like it out there. It wasn't any fun being lost."

"I won't either," I said. "I don't fit through the tunnel."

Pandora gave me a hard look.

"What about the Shadow Man?" I said.

Pandora raised her eyebrows.

"The Shadow Man is *real*," Felicia said. "It's not just something we imagined, Pandora; it's not just some man. It was across the street watching the bookstore almost all night. When I was following it, sometimes it was completely solid, but other times it would start to get see-through, as if it were made out of smoke or fog. It went down an alley just before the sun came up and got inside of a big box outside of a back doorway. I think that's where it hides. It's the sort of big box our new refrigerator came in."

"We decided last night that Dr. Malpin probably didn't send it," I said. "I read all about Dr. Malpin on the internet. He probably wouldn't know about the kinds of things that are in Garmund Firth's book."

Felicia's eyes got very wide. All of a sudden she had a look on her face as if she'd just seen the mouse.

"What?" I said, watching her closely.

"What was happening the first time you saw it, Rachel?"

"*You* remember," I said. "It was raining. I was looking out the window. You and Pandora were sitting on the carpet, and Pandora was reading from the book she couldn't remember having . . ."

I stopped. Suddenly I was hearing those odd words and seeing Garmund Firth's strange diagram in my head.

Maybe it wasn't only *people* who tended to miss the obvious.

"The diagram!" I said. "It's not just a picture! It was put inside the book to *do* something!"

Pandora's little forehead crease was back.

"When you read that strange part of the book to me," Felicia explained, "Rachel first saw the shadow. Then, when

129

you read part of the book to Rachel, the shadow started getting more solid." Felicia tilted her head to one side. "Don't you see, Pandora?"

I was pretty sure that Pandora was actually following all of this, but she didn't like where it was going.

"Maybe things are a lot more like that movie than you think they are," I said.

Pandora didn't say a word. She gave us each a stern look and then got up from the table and went downstairs to tend to the bookstore. After a minute Felicia and I followed, but we were careful to keep out of Pandora's way. We sat on the ledge to watch out the front window.

Overhead the sky was clear for a change; the street was very bright, though clouds rising up from down on the horizon suggested that a storm might be coming later. The leaves on the maple tree had turned bright yellow. A lot of them were scattered over the sidewalk. We both looked but we didn't see the Shadow Man anywhere. Maybe when you're partly see-through you don't like the bright sunlight.

After a while, Pandora went back upstairs. I saw the light on the telephone beside the cash register blink on, so I knew she was talking to someone on the bedroom extension. I wondered about that. When she came downstairs again she had the Garmund Firth book with her. She sat down on her favorite reading chair, which is the big leather one.

"Andy is coming over for pizza later," she casually announced.

Felicia and I exchanged glances.

"He'll be here a little after eight," Pandora said. "I want you both to be on your very best behavior."

This was certainly out of the blue. It was what you might call *a startling new development.*

130

"We need to thank him for bringing Felicia home," Pandora said. She raised her eyebrows in a challenging way. I'm sure she expected us to say something.

We didn't. We were being nonchalant.

"Well," Pandora said. She looked from one of us to the other. "OK, then." After a moment she gave a little shrug and opened the book.

A minute or two went by.

"Pandora?" I said.

Pandora quickly glanced up at me.

"Read us the last part of the book again," I said. "Not the hand-written part; the part just before that. Felicia was asleep when you read it to me earlier."

I'm sure that wasn't what Pandora was ready to argue about. She made a pouting expression and closed the book and reopened it from the back. I caught a glimpse of the strange diagram with its odd words and symbols, and of the long, hand-written entry. In the bright sunlight, the yellow-brown ink seemed even more faded than it had before.

Pandora flipped back through a few pages and looked at the header. "*Banishment: on the Dissolution of Thought Forms*," she read. "Is that it?"

"That's it," I said.

Pandora sighed—a sigh of resignation, I suppose you would call it. Then she began to read.

On Our Best Behavior

Around half-past seven Pandora ordered our pizza. She called *Panzolli's*, which is just across the old iron bridge. You can see the top of the bridge over the raggedy bushes from our back upstairs windows. Felicia told Pandora that she should ask for delivery, pointing out that Andy might show up early and find the door locked, and that it was clearly going to rain again. While it did look like rain, we actually didn't want Pandora going out to get it.

Just before eight our pizza arrived. It was extra-large. By then it was raining, and beginning to get cold and quite windy besides. Pandora paid the delivery man and closed the front door and took the box upstairs. Felicia and I had already had our dinner, but we followed close behind. We could smell the piece with our special toppings.

Pandora opened the kitchen drawer where she keeps the sharp knives and took out the corkscrew. She set the table with her best plates and wine glasses, and put out cloth napkins and some of her good silverware.

Felicia and I thought this was all a bit extravagant for pizza. Usually Pandora just carries the box into the living room and plops it down on the coffee table in front of the sofa.

Pandora had also made a salad. I really couldn't imagine a salad impressing anyone, but people are very odd about some of the things that they like to eat.

Preparations made, we all went into the living room and sat on the sofa to wait.

Around a quarter after eight we heard the door buzzer down in the bookstore and we all jumped up. Felicia and I would have run downstairs if Pandora hadn't told us we should wait. I suppose we'd caught her anticipation. The whole business of Andy's visit was getting quite interesting.

We heard Andy and Pandora talking down in the bookstore for a minute, and then we heard footsteps on the stairs.

Andy looked in through the kitchen doorway. "Hi," he said. I'd never seen Andy without his UPS uniform before. He was wearing blue jeans and a sweater and had an old leather jacket that was wet with the rain.

Pandora showed Andy around our apartment. He got *The Grand Tour.* He asked Pandora about our antique dresser and our Black Forest cuckoo clock, and admired some of the old Japanese prints that we have on the walls. (One of them that I especially like has cats in it.) I could tell he was truly interested and not just pretending to be.

After a while, Pandora mentioned that the pizza might be getting cold. Andy followed her into the kitchen. Pandora sat him down at the table. I heard the refrigerator door open and the cork pop out of the wine bottle. Since Felicia and I were being on our best behavior, but weren't entirely sure what that actually was, we waited in the living room while they had their salads. We decided that we had waited long enough when we heard the pizza box open.

Pandora took our special piece out of the box and put it on a saucer. She put the saucer on the floor between our dishes. Felicia likes anchovies, but I think they're much too salty. I like sausage and black olives.

Pandora went back to her chair. She was smiling to herself, probably thinking at that point that things were going especially well.

Felicia heard it first. She looked up, and then I heard it too.

"*Pandora!*" I whispered. "Did you leave the door unlocked?"

Andy caught Pandora's look and followed her eyes. His eyebrows went up when he saw Felicia. Her fur was as bushy as an angry raccoon's.

That's when we heard an enormous *CRASH!* downstairs. Pandora jumped and nearly spilled her wine and Andy got straight to his feet.

"The front door blew open," Pandora said, getting up

herself. "I probably forgot to lock it. Sometimes the latch doesn't catch." She touched Andy on the shoulder and he sat back down. She shot us a warning look and started for the stairs. We ignored it. We hurried to get ahead of her.

Halfway down we stopped, listening for the tiniest suspicious noise. The front door was standing wide. Wind was gusting along the street and wet, yellow leaves had blown in, leaving a scattered trail across the floor.

"You *see*?" Pandora said. She went on down.

Andy's voice carried down from the kitchen doorway: "Everything OK?"

"Everything's fine!" Pandora yelled back. She closed the front door and locked it.

Felicia had gone to the window to look out. I glanced nervously around the bookstore and then jumped up on the ledge beside her. We looked up and down the sidewalk and across the street toward the lamp post. There was nothing to see out there but wind and rain and flying leaves.

"Satisfied?" Pandora whispered. She shook her head and started for the stairs. Felicia and I exchanged glances and followed, trying our best to appear contrite. *Contrite* doesn't come easily for cats. We quietly went back to our pizza.

Felicia and I were both very curious about what might happen with Andy and Pandora. After dinner they went into the living room and we sat out of sight around the corner in the hallway, listening. Not much happened. They just talked and had another glass of wine and listened to some music for a while, and then Andy noticed the time and said he should probably go because he had to work early tomorrow. He put on his coat and went downstairs and Pandora went with him. Felicia got up to follow.

"No!" I said.

"Why not?"

I gave her a knowing look.

"Oooh," Felicia said.

After a while we heard the front door open and close again. Pandora came back and began clearing the table. She fetched the wine glasses from the living room and washed and dried everything and put it all away.

After a while we went to bed. Rain was beating against the windows; the iron radiator was making those quiet little sounds it makes when the furnace in the basement wakes up. Pandora opened an old book of English poetry. After a moment she began to read in that special way she has.

I closed my eyes to listen, and without even realizing it I began to fall asleep. Pandora's voice grew distant, and then what she was reading became part of the dream I was having. In my dream there was a girl who lived in a castle on an island in a river. The girl looked a lot like Pandora. There was a magic mirror the girl looked into, where she saw things going on in the outside world that for some reason she couldn't be part of. It was all very real, like a little movie playing inside my head.

"Pandora?" Felicia said.

I opened my eyes as Pandora looked up from her book.

"We didn't mess up tonight, did we?"

"No," Pandora said. She scratched the back of Felicia's head and Felicia closed her eyes. "You were both fine. But you've got to get over this business about the Shadow Man. You've both let your imaginations run away with you."

I thought about that, and about how real the dream of just a moment before had seemed.

"Andy's nice," Pandora said after a moment. "Don't you think?"

We both agreed that he was.

135

Pandora smiled, and then the smile turned into a yawn. She closed the book and put it on the nightstand, on top of the book by Garmund Firth. She switched off the bedside lamp and turned onto her side and pulled the covers up close under her ear.

A Child's Book of Blood

Felicia and I slept for a while. I woke up when I heard Felicia quietly jump to the floor and I got up too. We stopped in the kitchen for some water, and then we started down the stairs to the bookstore.

Midway down, we froze.

The wind was still blowing. Rain was streaming down the bottom of the front window. The light across the street cast long, rippling shadows across floor. In the big oxblood leather reading chair was the dark silhouette of a man.

We hurried back up to the kitchen, as quickly and quietly as only cats can.

"*It's him!*" Felicia said.

My heart was hammering. "How did he get in? The front door is locked!"

"We were *stupid!*" Felicia said. "*He was already in!*"

He had gotten in when the door had blown open, of course. He'd hidden in the basement or the storeroom.

"What should we do?" Felicia said. She was already close to panic. We needed to do something quickly.

"Go wake up Pandora!" I said. "Tell her the Shadow Man is downstairs!"

Felicia didn't move.

"*Now!*" I hissed.

She disappeared.

I crept partway back down the staircase, hiding in the

shadows. The Shadow Man was still in the chair. Behind me, I heard Pandora's sleepy voice upstairs in the bedroom. "It's 3 o'clock in the morning," she was saying. Then the nightstand lamp went on.

Some of the light reached down the stairs to where I was hiding. The Shadow Man's head slowly turned. I sprinted up the steps to the kitchen.

Pandora was just coming in barefooted, tying her robe. She was *really* pissed. "You two have *totally* flipped your lids," she said to me.

"Do you think so, Pandora? Do you really think so? *He's down there.*"

Pandora gave me *the look.* She was going to resolve this once and for all. She shot right past me and charged straight down the steps. Then she came back up the stairs just as quickly. Her face was pale. She hurried to the bedroom and came back flipping her cell phone open. It didn't beep. She gave it a disgusted look.

"Stay here!" she said.

Felicia and I exchanged a glance. *Not much chance of that.* As soon as Pandora was through the door we followed along right behind her.

On the bottom step, Pandora flipped on the lights.

He was still in the chair, turned in profile, just staring off into space. His face was pale, his eyes as black as obsidian. His lank black hair was wet with rain and hung down to a stiff white collar. Everything else was black: frock coat, waistcoat, trousers and riding boots. It was the look of an earlier time—like a picture of an early 19th Century English poet in one of our old books. It alarmed me as I realized just how big he was. Standing, he would surely be well over six feet tall.

"I called the police," Pandora announced, moving the

137

hand holding the phone. I knew she hadn't, because the cell phone's battery was dead and she hadn't gone back into the bedroom, but it still seemed like a good thing to say.

The Shadow Man's reaction wasn't particularly dramatic. There was, in fact, no reaction at all.

"*His name*," I whispered.

Pandora quickly glanced down at me.

"You *know* what it is, Pandora. *Say* it!"

Pandora looked back up. "Garmund . . . Firth?"

At first there was nothing. Then the Shadow Man blinked a couple of times, as if he were coming out of a trance. His head slowly turned toward the sound. A moment passed, and his eyes found Pandora, and then there was a single, almost imperceptible nod.

"Maybe you should get the book," I whispered.

Pandora looked uncertain, but she turned and went up the steps. I heard her in the bedroom. Then I heard her footsteps in the kitchen. I thought I heard a drawer open and shut. Another moment passed. When she returned, she had the book in her hand.

The book instantly drew the Shadow Man's eyes like a magnet. His long pale fingers slowly tightened on the arms of the chair. Leather squeaked and wood creaked. It terrified me to think how strong those hands must be.

Pandora moved cautiously toward the reading chair nearest the stairway door. Her eyes didn't leave the Shadow Man for an instant. As she sat down, Felicia and I slipped around to the floor on either side of her.

There we all were, facing one another from comfortable leather chairs across an old Oriental rug. If there had been a fireplace—and if the man opposite us hadn't looked quite so much like a vampire—it might have made for a cozy little Victorian picture.

"You *can't* be Garmund Firth," Pandora said slowly.

The Shadow Man's eyes shifted to Pandora's face. Taking his eyes away from the book seemed to be very difficult for him.

"Garmund Firth—the man who wrote this—has been dead nearly one hundred and fifty years."

Wheels were beginning to turn. The head moved slightly; the thin lips twitched; and then a voice spoke that made me shiver: "You are telling me that . . . I am a *ghost?*"

"I'm not sure *what* you are," Pandora said. "*Garmund Firth* was an occultist. There's something he put inside this book: a sort of diagram. There's a long, handwritten passage that . . . might be some sort of incantation." She nervously shifted the book on her lap. "All *we* did was read it. Anything that happened was an accident."

"*We?*" The Shadow Man raised his eyebrows. He took us all in, and then his gaze settled back on Pandora. "What are *you*, then, to be having such *accidents?*"

"That's something else that I'm not entirely sure of."

"Ah. I see." The Shadow Man tilted his head to one side. "Yet here I am—purposely invited or not." His hands were working against the chair arms now in a most distressing fashion. "How . . . *awkward* for you."

"This is *bad*," Felicia whispered urgently. "We should run upstairs! Pandora could lock the door behind us. We could do that banishing thing! Maybe we could send him away!"

"Away *where?*" I said.

"What does it matter, Rachel? *How does that matter at all?* He'd be gone!"

Pandora had heard, I knew, but she gave no sign of it. The Shadow Man hadn't heard a thing. "We're not insensitive to your situation," Pandora offered.

"YOU KNOW *NOTHING* OF MY SITUATION!"

Pandora flinched. Felicia almost bolted. For a lingering moment, the only sounds were the wind and the rain.

"What . . ." Pandora paused and swallowed. "What do you want?"

She was trying to stay in control of the situation—I could see that—but it clearly wasn't going so well.

"*Want*?" The Shadow Man's long fingers extended wide, palms flat on the chair arms. The hands slowly closed again. "Blood in my veins? A beating heart to pump it? *Memories*, perhaps? Something—*anything*—to fill my mind, in place of these . . . terrifying *compulsions*." He leaned forward in his chair and a dark tendril of hair fell across his face. Abruptly he shifted to a pleasant, conversational tone, completely at odds with the intensity of his expression: "For some reason that I simply cannot fathom, the thought of blood obsesses me. I think of it . . . almost . . . constantly."

"Rachel!" Felicia whispered desperately. *"RACHEL!"*

I was ignoring her. I was frantically trying to sort something out: What *was* it about the blood?

"We might be able to . . . to undo what we did," Pandora said, a tremor in her voice now. From the corner of my eye I saw her hand moving cautiously toward the pocket of her bathrobe. I remembered that she'd stopped in the kitchen. My heart skipped a beat as I thought of the knife drawer.

The Shadow Man's eyes were fixed on Pandora's face. "Ah," he said. "I *see*." His lips slowly composed themselves into a thin, tight smile, but for just an instant I thought I'd seen them tremble. "I'm sure you'll understand why your offer might not . . . appeal to me."

Thoughts were flying through my head now like leaves on the street outside: Thoughts of a faded violet pressed inside a book, and of the traces of a girl that it had carried;

of yellowish-brown ink that wasn't really ink at all, and of how words and symbols drawn with it well over a century before had faded as the Shadow Man had grown more solid.

Time seemed to slow. I had almost glimpsed the pattern. Then, quite suddenly, all of the pieces fell into place. Suddenly I understood.

I took a deep breath. "There might be another way," I said.

"What?" Pandora looked down at me. "What other way, Rachel?"

"We have to finish what we started," I said. "Don't you see what's wrong with him, Pandora? Part of him is *missing*. It's what draws him here. *It's still inside the book.*"

"*NO!*" Felicia said. "That's *crazy*, Rachel! We'll just make things worse!"

I looked at her. "It might have been an accident, Felicia, but he's here because of us. *The same way that we're here because of Dr. Malpin.*"

Felicia locked eyes with me. "So?"

"Do you remember the terrible thing that Dr. Malpin was going to do?" I gave her a moment to remember. "Well, *we* have to be *better* than that."

Outside, the wind gusted. Rain pelted the glass of the big front window. Pandora looked down at the book on her lap, and then she looked up at the Shadow Man. Her hand moved away from her pocket.

"There might be a way we can help," she said.

* * *

The Shadow Man took the book with him when he left. That, of course, was exactly as it should have been.

I looked at the book for a final time before he left with it—after we had formed our circle, and read the words, and closed our eyes, and imagined together how things should be so clearly that when we opened them again, that's how things really were.

Every symbol and word drawn or written in yellowish-brown had vanished without a trace. It had been the ink, of course—the blood of the book's long-dead author—that had carried the vital traces across the years.

Who knows how? Not me. I'm only telling you that it was so. But is it any less strange to think that everything that makes a cat or a king rides on an invisible bit of DNA?

When magic really works—and it sometimes does—it's probably just science not yet figured out. That's what *I* think.

My advice is to keep an open mind.

Cookies and Coins

I like to watch the snow from the bookstore window. That's what I was doing one morning when I spied a familiar figure coming up the street, black coat flapping in the wind. It paused by the lamp post, waited for a car to pass, and crossed toward the door. "We have company," I said.

Pandora was stringing lights on our Christmas tree. Felicia was watching. They both looked around as the bells on the door jingled and snowflakes swirled in on a rush of cold December air. Garmund—who wasn't quite so pale these days but still looked more than a little sinister—stomped his boots and shook the snow off his coat.

"It's cold," he said.

"It's winter," Pandora replied. Technically it wasn't yet, but this year the weather had gotten ahead of the calendar.

Pandora backed down the stepladder and stood off from the tree a bit, examining it with a critical eye. She and Andy had brought it in the night before. The whole bookstore smelled of pine.

"We haven't seen you for a while, Garmund," Pandora said.

"Sorry." He studied the cookies on the tray beside the cash register and selected one. "Been busy."

Pandora adjusted a Christmas tree light to a higher branch. "Doing what?"

"Acquiring an identity, among other things. Simply being present in the modern world is apparently insufficient; one must also possess the correct bits of paper and plastic."

Pandora glanced at Garmund. "You can manage that?"

"Already done so." He discarded half of the first cookie and selected another. "As it turns out, I'm terribly clever. Probably make a wonderfully capable criminal. Were I so inclined," he added archly.

The little crease showed on Pandora's forehead for a moment. "Where are you staying?"

"Across the river," he replied. "Do you know Baldwin's Music Store? I'm in the apartment above that."

"Surely that must cost something . . ."

"You're a suspicious sort of a woman, Pandora Fox." Garmund took something from a coat pocket. He flicked his thumb. There was a golden glint in the air and Pandora deftly caught it.

"A Victoria sovereign?" she said, looking up.

"You either gave it to me or returned it; which, I suppose, is a deep metaphysical puzzle."

As though he weren't himself, I thought.

"There were fifty hidden in the boards of the book. My namesake prepared for the future." He nodded toward the coin. "I'd be pleased if you kept that. As a little memento."

Pandora smiled. "What will you do, Garmund?"

143

"Still sorting that out. Lately I've become something of a fixture over at the public library. I've had a bit of catching up to do."

"You can always come here, Pandora said. "We *do* have books."

"I might." He glanced around the store. "You seem to have an uncommon selection—particularly on certain esoteric topics that have caught my attention of late."

"What's he talking about?" Felicia whispered to me.

Garmund glanced toward Felicia, almost as though he'd heard something. She tilted her head to one side and gazed back curiously. After a momentary staring contest they called it a draw.

"Well," he announced, "I must be off." He turned his collar up. "Someone's coming to install a cable. *I* am getting high-speed internet."

Pandora held up the hand with the coin. "Thanks, Garmund. Don't be a stranger."

The former Shadow Man bowed formally, his eyes taking us all in. "Ladies." Then the door opened and closed and he was gone.

Pandora flipped the coin into the air and caught it. She stuck it into her pocket. Then she took a tissue-covered ornament from a box and began to unwrap it.

Felicia jumped down off the counter. She looked up at Pandora. "That's a bit odd, don't you think?"

"What's odd?" Pandora asked, absently.

"That someone from the 19th Century would want an internet connection," Felicia said.

Pandora gave Felicia a long and thoughtful look. Her eyes shifted to me. After a moment she slowly shook her head. Then she turned back to decorating the tree.

STORE HOURS
MON-FRI   9 am to 6 pm
SATURDAY   9 am to 8 pm
SUNDAY   CLOSED

ABOUT THE AUTHOR

G. S. Hargrave lives and works in a northwest Indiana lake cottage. His earliest professional writing, which fell into the popular mystery genre, first appeared in the United States, Germany, and Japan some 25 years ago. These days he's writing fantasy and science fiction. He's also an artist and an improvisational guitarist.